THE K[...[ ]TERY SERIES

Joanna Campbell Slan

~Spot On Publishing~

Joanna Campbell Slan
Spot On Publishing, a division of Luminary LLC
9307 SE Olympus Street
Hobe Sound, FL 33455 USA
http://www.SpotOnPublishing.org

Book Layout © 2016 http://www.BookDesignTemplates.com
Covers by Dar Albert, Wicked Smart Designs
http://www.WickedSmartDesigns.com
The Zentangle® art form and method was created by Rick Roberts and Maria Thomas, and is copyrighted. Zentangle® is a registered trademark of Zentangle, Inc. Learn more at http://www.zentangle.com.
Editing by Wendy Green
ISBN 13: 978-154209990
ISBN: 1543209998
Revised 08/25/2017

INK, RED, DEAD

BOOK #3 IN
THE KIKI LOWENSTEIN MYSTERY SERIES

CHAPTER 1

Mid-August/Ladue, Missouri
Early Thursday morning

"The minute we pulled into the driveway, I told Clancy this was a bad idea. A very, very bad idea. I had this yucky feeling. Be sure to put that in the report." I pointed at the pad where Detective Stan Hadcho of the St. Louis Police Department took notes. His pen moved across the pad. A slight breeze lifted a strand of his jet black hair. Instinctively, I leaned forward to see if I could catch a little of the fresh air. But it was no use. The atmosphere was thick with nasty smells. Even the walnut table where we had gathered around had its own funky stink. I could hear myself wheezing as my lungs struggled to cope.

"That so? You thought it was a bad idea. And you are?" His voice was muffled by the tissues he'd stuffed up his nose.

"I'm Kiki Lowenstein. This is my friend Clancy Whitehead. We work together at Time in a Bottle, that's a scrapbook store south of 40, right off of Brentwood Boulevard. When we got here, I had a bad feeling."

A dribble of sweat ran down the cop's temple. The backs of his hands gleamed with perspiration. A ring of wet spread out from his neck along his collar, but he didn't loosen his tie. That's self-discipline for you. Even in the blazing heat of a mid-August day in Missouri, this man managed to look like a natty dresser.

Clancy huddled in her chair, trying not to touch any of the gross surfaces that surrounded us. I met Clancy shortly after she and her husband split up. Back then, a full day for her was alphabetizing her spice rack. She hated her life. When I suggested that she help us out at Time in a Bottle, Clancy jumped on the change. Since then, she's proven herself to be an invaluable part-time employee who's always willing to come in at the last minute and work. Although she's not much of a crafter, she's learning. She's highly organized, a trait that's not part of my DNA. If I'm being totally honest, I'm glad to have Clancy around because my boss, Dodie, also hired another part-timer, Bama Vess. To say that Bama and I don't get along would be to put a nice spin on our relationship. I don't like her, and she doesn't like me. I think I have good reason. Bama acts like she's hot stuff, and she's always taking time off. For example, she couldn't come to the crop at Marla's house. Bama said she was "busy."

Busy my big butt.

Bama doesn't like leaving the store.

"You had a bad feeling," Hadcho repeated, more to himself than to us.

"Right. I'm a card-carrying Episcopalian, high church, but I respect the power of intuition. We should have turned around and gone home. Back to the store."

Clancy was trembling so hard that her chair was clacking against the table. She fluffed her hair and re-applied her bright red Chanel lipstick. It was a reflexive action; her attempt at regaining control. Unfortunately her hand shook like a tree in a tornado and as a result, she definitely had colored out of the lines. It might have been comical under other circumstances. Not today.

"Your business is actually in Richmond Heights, not St. Louis proper, and the two of you are here, why?" Hadcho kept writing.

"Because we were supposed to hold a scrapbook party here. We call them crops," I said.

"Really?" Hadcho raised his eyebrows and scanned the stacks of newspapers that were stacked high, forming tattered gray walls around us. Although we were sitting in a dining room, the only indication of its intended use was a round wooden table with four chairs. We occupied three of the seats. A big calico cat calmly washed her paws as she sat on the fourth seat.

"Why would you hold an event here?" The cop wondered. "Doesn't seem like the sort of image anyone would want to project to their customers."

He was right. This place was a total dump. A disaster. A mess. Actually, there weren't enough negative adjectives in my vocabulary to cover it.

Clancy and I work for Dodie Goldfader, the owner of Time in a Bottle. Her store is considered by many to be the premier scrapbook store in the Midwest. Dodie has high standards, sometimes impossibly so. But to make a long story short: Dodie had decreed we'd do off-site events. So Clancy and I were here at Marla Lever's house to put on a scrapbook party while Marla played hostess.

That was the plan.

The reality was different. One look at the unkempt state of the place told us something was seriously amiss. On closer inspection…well…my "spidey" senses went on full alert. I opened my phone and dialed 911. Hadcho had been a few blocks away in his police cruiser.

"Detective? I'll stand outside and tell people the scrapbook event has been called off. That okay? Drat." Clancy paused midway in returning her Chanel lipstick to her purse. She held up the white bag for our inspection. "Just look at this ink stain. Soaked right through the leather. The pen I was carrying must have come uncapped. Shoot, and I really like this purse."

The pen had also jabbed through the leather and doodled on her nice white slacks. I decided not to tell her because there was nothing she could do about it, and I figured that she was already shook up. Why make things worse? But every step she took caused her purse to swing forward and back, like a pendulum, and another navy blue ink smear decorated the hip of her white slacks.

"No drycleaner on earth will ever get that out," Hadcho said.

"Those are linen. Nice stuff."

The man knew his fabrics. I waited until Clancy had walked away before telling Hadcho, "I wanted to turn around and go home. Really I did. I knew something was wrong." Was I ever right about wrong.

"Next time that happens, pay attention," said Hadcho, pointing a pen at me. "Because your instincts were right, and now you've stepped in a mess."

"You mean because Marla is a hoarder?"

"No, because you have poop on your shoes." Hadcho glanced down at my Keds. "How about if you clean those off? We're going to be here a while."

CHAPTER 2

"Start at the beginning," Hadcho said. "Had you ever been here before?"

"Nope," we answered in chorus.

"What did you see when you first arrived?"

"We saw this...this...garbage dump," said Clancy. "We double-checked the address, and then we tried to track down the woman we were here to meet."

"Marla," I added, "Marla Lever." With that, I took over telling the story...

"I wonder if her car's here," I had said to Clancy as we trooped through the grass. We'd already tried knocking at the front door and calling. Now we waded toward the detached garage, waving away the smoke signals of bugs that flew up in our wake.

Cupping our hands around our eyes, we pressed our faces to the dirty window. We could barely make out Marla Lever's car. Old furniture, lawn chairs, tools, and gadgets were stuffed around a shiny gold Impala with a cream colored leather roof. A dank smell oozed from the building.

"What do you think?" Clancy turned to me.

"She has to be here. Her car is."

"Unless someone gave her a ride somewhere."

"Who would do that?" asked Clancy. We both knew that Marla was a loner. I'd never seen her come into our store with friends.

Nor had I seen her leave with buddies. In fact, I'd never heard her talk about people at all.

"You don't think she got confused, do you? Maybe she thought the scrapbook event was going to be held at the store? When did you last talk?"

"Yesterday. I said we'd be here early. She seemed a little

nervous."

"No kidding? Wonder why." Clancy usually isn't sarcastic, but she had agreed with me that moving scrapbook events from one customer's house to the next was a bad idea.

"She was going to try to get someone to come mow her grass."

"That 'someone' gave up."

"Obviously." I scratched at a spot behind my knee. Tick bite. I just knew it. A trickle of perspiration ran down my face.

"You figure she bailed on us? Maybe when she couldn't get the grass cut?"

"I have no idea." Crickets sang lustily in the grass, falling silent as we walked nearer.

"Call her again."

I opened my cell phone, redialed Marla's number, and listened. This time we heard ringing in the house.

"Up to you." Clancy faked a tap dance, waved her arms and sang, "Shall we stay or shall we go? Da-da-da-ta-da-da-ta."

That Clancy. What a card. I shook an ant off my sleeve and weighed our options.

We could go back to the store. That meant facing Rebekkah the Terrible, Dodie's daughter, our new "Sales Mangler." (Yes, that's what her business cards said. I didn't bother to point out the typo.)

Or we could sit in Clancy's car, crank up the A/C and wait, hoping Marla would show up. Maybe she was out running errands and got behind.

Errands on foot? In this heat? I was dreaming, wasn't I? Or we could leave. That nagging voice in my head suggested we hightail it.

But we couldn't leave. Twelve people had RSVPed, promising to join us here in forty-five minutes for a crop. We would have to try to head those scrappers off. At the very least, we needed to post a message on the front door.

Clancy noticed the pained expression on my face.

"The scrapbookers aren't going to like this," I said.

"We could stand at Marla's door and pretend to be knocking when the others drive up," she said, in a voice that was oh-so casual. "This whole fiasco would look like a surprise to us, which it is."

"We could both look pitiful," I added.

I had practice at that. I do "pitiful" pretty well. "That way maybe they'd blame Marla. Not us."

Sounds petty, but I did not want to get blamed for cancelling this crop. I know from experience that scrapbookers do not take kindly to such disappointments. Loading up all their gear is a lot of work. Excitement runs high at scrapbooking events. Tempers naturally follow at a fevered pitch. Furthermore, we'd had to turn down customers who wanted to come once they heard I was teaching a class on how to incorporate newspapers as a journaling device on their scrapbook and journal pages. In fact, we'd titled the crop: What's Black and White and Read All Over Your Pages?

Since it was summer in St. Louis, and the Cards were winning, everyone wanted to incorporate their exploits into their scrapbook albums. My nifty idea did just that. Now all my supplies were sitting in the trunk of Clancy's car—and the crop looked like it was a non-starter.

"Drat." That was all I could muster. I'd lobbied long and loud against this traveling "dog and pony" show. I'm a control freak. I liked having events in the store because I could predict the environment. When you go to someone's home, you never know if they'll have a proper work space, good lighting, and so on. Or if they'll have a rambunctious dog or an ailing live-in relative or a backed up toilet.

Could happen.

Huh. It *had* happened.

Louise Hudson had a dachshund who couldn't stop piddling with joy at our arrival. Ekla Guitano's father-in-law insisted on sitting with us to watch what we were doing—and managed to fart at regular intervals. But the worst mess had been Kathi Zantini's toilet. It overflowed, sending a tsunami of sewage into the family room where we were crafting.

All those nightmares had come to pass. But not a no-show. Not yet. But I knew it might.

We were bound to wind up at someone's house and discover she had the wrong date on her calendar. I warned Dodie of impending doom, while her daughter Rebekkah glowered at me.

Don't get me wrong. I love Rebekkah. But she's totally unsuited for the job of being our store manager. She's not detail oriented, she's not mature enough to manage people, and she's not willing to listen. Furthermore, her new title totally went to her head. Rather than hearing me out, Rebekkah dug in her heels. (Whatever that means.) The off-site events were her idea and she was not about to listen to reason.

Of course, Bama sided with Rebekkah. That woman is such a brown-noser that she had the nerve to say, "I think going to people's houses is a wonderful idea. Very ingenious."

That was rich, considering how she always managed to get out of being the person who handled the off-site, at-home crops.

I wasn't about to give in easily even if Bama's comment did make me look like a chump. "I don't think this is a good idea. We have customers with mega-bucks and customers who shoot bucks for food. There's too much of an economic disparity in our clientele to pull this off. Someone is bound to feel bad. Or feel slighted. Get embarrassed."

"Thanks for the warning, Sunshine," Dodie gave me a smile that wasn't a smile. Not really. "I think Rebekkah came up with a good idea. I'm supporting her with it. In the immortal words of Jean Luc Piccard, 'Make it so.'"

To that Rebekkah added a self-satisfied smirk. Not her best look. Bama gave Dodie a high five. I tried not to sulk.

Boy, was I eager to get back to the store and tell them how this "super" idea had backfired.

CHAPTER 3

With less than an hour to go before the crop started, Clancy and I were starting to get desperate – and wilted. Our clothing was damp with stinky sweat.

"Maybe Marla's in the bathroom." Clancy sounded optimistic. "That happens when people get nervous."

"Right. A bathroom in Boliva. I bet she left the country."

"Kiki Lowenstein, you are such a goof."

"No, I'm being honest. You know, and I know, Marla didn't want to host this. I could tell she wanted out of this…but Rebekkah…"

"Yes, exactly. 'But Rebekkah.' We've been saying that a lot lately, haven't we?"

"Rebekkah refused to take no for an answer. Marla tried to get out of it, but Rebekkah pushed her. So, how could Marla save face? She could run away." Sounded reasonable to me. I wanted to run away. Right now.

"Without her car?"

"She could run far away. Very, very far away." A dreamy series of tropical scenes danced through my head. "You don't need your car if you cross the ocean. Do you know that if you MapQuest directions from Los Angeles to Honolulu it says, 'Kayak across Pacific Ocean – 2756 miles?' If you go from Japan to China on MapQuest, the directions say 'jet ski across the Pacific Ocean – 762 km?'"

Clancy stared at me from under her thick black lashes. "Kiki Lowenstein, you have entirely too much time on your hands."

"No, really! It's all true. Maybe she decided to try it. Whatcha think? Jet ski or kayak? Hmm? Could we just leave? Put a note on the door and try to contact the others?"

"Sounds good to me." Clancy, clearly wilting, reached inside her leather handbag. As she hauled out her keys, we looked at each other in silence, both of us feeling guilty.

That's when it hit me. "Wait a minute! Do you hear anything?"

"Other than the happy hum of mosquitoes as they make withdrawals from my blood bank? No. I don't hear a thing. Why?"

I turned in a small circle, listening carefully. There was no noise. Not a whirl or a humming or a clank. The air conditioner was suspiciously quiet. Given the heat, that didn't make sense.

"What?" Clancy jingled the keys at me. "Can we go?"

"There's no noise. How come the air conditioning isn't going? Huh? What if she's here? Inside? What if her A/C went out, and she's sick? Or…worse?"

"The news," Clancy whispered and turned pale.

Every broadcast of the evening news brought more and more reports of elderly people found dead at home. The culprit? The soaring temps. A nasty heat wave had wrestled the Midwest to the mat. The city and the county of St. Louis both were ready to cry, "Uncle!" Cooling shelters were filled to capacity. Neighbors had been asked to check on each other. Hazardous situations were to be reported to authorities.

I had sighed then, giving up a gust of capitulation. "Come on. We can't leave until we know she's okay. Let's try the front door again. After that, we call the cops."

That's when I jiggled the handle harder and put my shoulder against it. To my shock, the door opened slightly. A fetid stink oozed out at me. The smell nearly bowled me over. It was sickly sweet, rotten, and pervasive with an undertone of ammonia. I turned my head, gasping for air, and gagged.

"Ugh!" Clancy had put her hand over her mouth and coughed.

"What is that smell? Cat pee?"

A dozen kitty faces filled the open space between door and door jam.

"I think so." Using the tip of my Keds to keep the cats from getting caught in the door, I had eased it shut. I didn't slam it, but I did close it enough that none of the kitties could race outside. The cats protested with loud meows, but there were no yelps of pain.

"Marla has to be in there. Why else would the door be unlocked?" Clancy said. "And if she's there. She's in trouble."

"I'm going in, but I'll need to move fast." I had gulped fresh air. I used my toe to nudge the cats back inside, hopped over the top of them (as a crowd had now gathered), and I slowly closed the door behind me. My eyes watered like garden hoses. I found it hard to take a breath, but I was on a mission, so I stepped further into the house—even though I couldn't see anything.

"Marla? Marla, it's Kiki! Remember? Clancy and I came early to help you get ready for the crop. Yoo-hoo? Anybody home?"

The room had started moving, coming toward me. A carpet of living cats. Big and small. Striped, yellow, black, white, Siamese, long-haired, short-haired, and practically no haired.

"Whoa." I backed up against the entrance as they crawled toward me, wave after wave of feline faces. I scanned the room, I felt disoriented, dizzy even, standing in a narrow tunnel formed by a towering piles of newspapers. The room closed in on me.

The heat in the house and the ammonia from the cat pee caused me to feel light-headed. My chest walls tightened, a prelude to an asthma attack. Between the smell and the heat, I couldn't function. At least, not very well.

"Marla? Marla!"

And the cats kept coming.

CHAPTER 4

Meowing and mewing and hissing, they pawed my legs. I plucked them off gently, and as soon as I untangled one, two more took its place. They reared back on their haunches and patted the air, trying to get my attention. They jumped over each other to get to me. They ran under each other. They rolled like the tumbleweeds you saw in Westerns.

"Marla? Hello?"

I thought I heard a noise, a human groan.

Or was it a cat?

I walked toward the sound, following a path of urine-soaked newspapers and nasty carpet samples. I tried not to step on paws or tails, but I didn't dare touch the makeshift walls of newspaper for balance out of fear they would come down on me. Twelve feet in, the tunnel widened into an open space where a sagging sofa faced a quiet TV. The cats hopped down from the top of the old fashioned television console to greet me, yowling at my feet and rubbing against my legs.

In the heart of the house, the heat became even more oppressive. I pulled up my shirt and held it over my face even though my tummy was exposed. I did my best to breathe through the fabric.

"Marla?"

I paused to listen.

Then I saw it: Marla's purse. The keys dangled half-in and half-out.

She wouldn't have left without it.

Couldn't have.

"Marla? Marla!" I stumbled over furry bodies, moving as fast as I could, keeping on the narrow pathway. I wandered through a rabbit warren of flattened and stacked cardboard boxes. I found myself surrounded by tall metal shelves, each crammed with stuff: cans, broken toys, clothing, broken appliances, and old paperback books. The smell of must and mold intensified the stink of cat pee.

I gagged but kept moving. "Marla? Marla, are you in here?"

I couldn't tell if I heard a noise or not. The cats' cries crescendoed to a loud cacophony of complaints. A crowd of cats, lean and hungry, kept pace with me. There were so many, I couldn't count them.

I came upon a once-beautiful round oak pedestal table marred by the scratch marks of dozens of claws. On the table top sat a dirty pet bed. Three cats slept there. Except that not all of them were sleeping. One was dead.

I had swallowed hard, tried not to heave, and retraced my steps.

"Mar-la!" I had yelled at the top of my voice. I couldn't take much more of this.

A moan beckoned me deeper into the dark house, a place where junk blocked all the light from the windows and fixtures.

"Marla!" I yelled again, coughing some as the fumes snatched the air from my lungs. The tightness in my chest cut off my wind, like a band tightening across my ribs.

"Uhhh." The noise came from the back of the house. It was human and it was in distress.

CHAPTER 5

The noise beckoned me, even though I didn't want to go farther inside. Following the faint moans, and instinct, I picked my way to what I assumed was a bedroom door. Summoning all my willpower, I pushed it open, only to spot a pair of legs hanging off the end of a bed.

"Marla?"

If she had not whimpered, I wouldn't have known she was alive.

Pushing cats out of the way, I ran to her and switched on a bedside lamp. Her skin felt clammy to my touch. I could see her heartbeat through the thin skin in her temple. She didn't appear to be bleeding. I was afraid to encourage her to sit up in case that might do her more harm than good.

There was a half a glass of water on a low dresser nearby. I dipped my fingers into it and applied it to her lips. She responded by licking the water off her mouth. I repeated the action until I'd gotten a quarter of the glass down her.

"Hang on, I'll get help." I raced out the way I'd come, hopping over cats as best I could. I threw the front door open so wide that it bumped Clancy on the backside.

"Oh," she moaned as she wiped her mouth. A sour smell in the air told me she'd been sick.

"Marla's in there."

"She okay?" Clancy burped quietly. "Excuse me."

"I'm calling in the Calvary." I fished in my purse for my phone. I also needed my inhaler. I could hear myself wheezing.

"That's cavalry, not Calvary." Clancy bent over the railing and heaved.

I dialed 911.

"My friend and I are okay, but we've got a situation here." I told the dispatcher our names, our address, and that we needed an ambulance immediately. The dispatcher asked me several questions about Marla's condition, and then, "Are you with the woman right now?"

"I'm not," and in disjointed sentences I explained how many cats there were in the house. "There are also stacks and stacks of newspapers, so it's like walking through a tunnel. A really, really narrow tunnel that might fall down at any time."

"We don't want you to endanger yourself," said the calm and collected voice on the other end. "Stay where you are. I have a detective in the area who's on his way. I'll also alert Animal Control."

"Good idea."

"Mrs. Lowenstein, is that you wheezing? If you are having trouble breathing, you need to get yourself into some place where there's air conditioning."

"I can't go sit in the car. Not when Marla's in such bad shape." Of course, that's what I tried to say. The truth is my asthma now rendered talking nearly impossible. I wheezed like a bad church organ. I raised a quizzical eyebrow at Clancy. "Can you go see about her?"

"Are you kidding?" My friend shook her head. "I can barely stand up. It's not smart for either of us to go inside. Remember those brothers who died in New York? Buried under all the junk they'd collected? With so many papers piled up, they could fall down on you. Us. That wouldn't do Marla any good, would it?"

CHAPTER 6

I agreed and searched in earnest for my inhaler. I found it at the bottom of my purse. I took one puff and watched Clancy get the dry heaves. When they stopped, she picked her way down the front steps to lean against the front of Marla's house. I took a second puff from my inhaler. I was exhaling slowly when a police cruiser came around the corner on two wheels.

"Detective Stan Hadcho," the driver said, as he flipped open his jacket to display a badge. He followed that by handing us both his card. "What's up?"

"There's a woman inside in distress. She's alive, but in a bad way—" I opened the door, but didn't step inside because the loud *yuga-yuga-yuga* of a siren split the air.

"Step aside." Hadcho bounded up the stairs and grabbed me by the arm. "Let the professionals do their jobs."

A bright yellow ambulance rolled to a stop behind Hadcho's car. The doors flew open and EMTs barreled out.

"Where?" The first one shouted at me.

"Straight back and to the left. In a bedroom, but you need to be careful —"

The first medic didn't wait for me to finish. He opened the door, cats came tumbling out of the house. The smell hit all of us and sent us reeling. The EMTs stepped over the animals and made their way inside.

Hadcho fisted his hands on his hips, watched as they disappeared, and shook his head. "I have a bad feeling about this."

CHAPTER 7

A cat got his tail caught in the door and let out an ear-splitting yowl. I helped Hadcho move the animal back into the house. In the process, we had to shoo away a herd of other felines, who were trying desperately to escape. I did everything I could to keep them from getting outside because I worried that they'd get hit by cars or whatever. I didn't want to contemplate what awful fates might intervene. Using his foot, Hadcho helped me nudge the kitties back inside the house.

"If he bites you, you're in trouble," said Clancy, when I chased after a big black cat. "I bet none of these have had rabies shots."

That worried me, but I wasn't about to let an animal get hurt on my watch.

After I corralled the big black cat—and he proved himself to be a lover, not a fighter—Hadcho said, "I need to take your statements. Let's go inside."

"Really?" I asked in disbelief. I couldn't believe he wanted to enter Marla's mess. "Okay, after you."

Hadcho led us to Marla's dining room. Clancy was pale as a sheet. She held a tissue over her nose. I tried to breathe through my mouth.

"Fresh air will help." Hadcho attacked one of the windows.

With a lot of effort, he managed to raise the sash. There wasn't much of a breeze, but we did get a smidgeon of relief from the outside air. At the detective's direction, Clancy and I took seats at Marla's dining room table. Hadcho shooed away the cats who were occupying the table top. Using the pet bed, he also picked up and removed the body of the cat that had crossed the rainbow bridge. Next Hadcho pulled a thin pack of wipes from an inside pocket and swept the table's surface clean. The reassuring scent of Lysol filled the air, but even that was overcome by the down-deep stink of the place. All three of us stuffed tissues up in our noses to dull the smell. Not that it helped much.

"What on earth convinced you to stick around?" he asked.

"Kiki wanted to turn around and go home. But Rebekkah Goldfader would have given us heck times three." Clancy shivered, despite the heat. Despite the tissues sticking out of her nose, but she somehow managed to look elegant. I have no idea how. I think she channeled Jackie Kennedy.

Clancy paused, glancing over at the pet bed and the dead body. "Why isn't that cat moving? Is it…?"

I looked more closely. "It's dead."

"Animal Control is on the way." Hadcho stared at his phone. He frowned and punched in a message to someone.

While he was occupied, I grabbed the offending pet bed and rolled it up. My intent was to carry it into another room, but before I could, Clancy ran past me. Even after the front door slammed shut, you could hear the faint sounds of her retching. Hadcho was busy with his phone, so I started to follow Clancy with my odiferous bundle in tow.

"Stop!" yelled Hadcho. "Ladies, both of you. Get back here. Now."

"I'll just put this outside," I said.

"No way. This might be a crime scene. I can't tell yet. Sit down and stay put." Hadcho went and found Clancy. "Both of you need to be where I can keep an eye on you."

"Do we have to?" Clancy wobbled her way back to the dining room table. She patted her mouth with a tissue. "Couldn't we wait outside?"

"I have to take your statements," said Hadcho. "It'll go faster if I have a surface to write on."

A knock at the door interrupted us again. Hadcho excused himself and returned with two Animal Control officers, a man and a woman. I showed the man the pet bed and asked him to deal with the dead cat first. Hadcho explained to the officers that the medics were still working on Marla back in her bedroom.

"This is ridiculous," said Hadcho, dabbing at his forehead. "Even with the window open, there's no air in here at all. Stay put."

Clancy and I did as we were told. In a few minutes, Hadcho came back with a box fan that he'd found stuffed in a closet. He pulled the sash up higher and stuck the box fan against the window screen. When he hit the switch, it roared to life.

"Ah," I said, as the breeze danced over my sweaty skin.

While Clancy and I answered Hadcho's questions, we watched the Animal Control officers round up kitties. On the reluctant ones, they used a catchpole. At first, most of the cats ran away. Watching the officers scurry around, I worried that they might knock over some of the piles of newspapers. Hadcho must have come to the same conclusion. His face glowered at the sight of the uniformed officers darting around the stacks of newspapers.

"You've got to find another way," Hadcho said. "You can't be chasing these animals around. It's not safe."

"They look to me like they're starving. Got any cat food?" I asked the Animal Control officer.

She opened a can of Little Friskies and stuck it in a big carrier.

In two seconds flat, she had a dozen cats fighting to climb aboard.

"Those poor animals." Clancy watched in horror. She isn't an animal lover like I am. That means, she's not nutty about critters. She's a good person. Kind and loving. She would never hurt an animal. She's just not too keen on dealing with the mess of owning one.

"I bet all these cats are dehydrated." I reached over, lightly pulled up the scruff of the neck of a tabby passing by. The fur stayed in an upright, tented position. "Yep. Definitely dehydrated. I'll just go into the kitchen and—"

"You will do no such thing. Sit. Stay." Hadcho frowned at me. "I need a report from both of you. I can't have you running around in this mess. What if one of these piles of papers comes down on you?"

As I scanned the walls of paper around us, a trickle of moisture inched its way between my boobs.

"Coming through." A couple of EMTs shuffled by, using their feet to sweep felines out of their way. They carried Marla on a stretcher, maneuvering their burden through the floor-to-ceiling stacks of newspapers. A third EMT followed, carrying a bag of saline and a tank of oxygen attached to our ailing friend.

Ignoring Hadcho's shouts to sit down, I tried to keep the animals from getting underfoot, but the cats were faster than I. More wily, too. Two of them made a beeline for the front door. I grabbed a piece of cardstock and used it as a makeshift gate to hold them back.

I was partially successful. Only one cat escaped. But the thundering herd of kitty paws had definitely gotten Hadcho's attention. He and Clancy both were trying to round up the escapees.

By my best guesstimate, there were at least one hundred and one felines. After the techs got by, I ran out to grab the cat who'd run past me and out the door, but it raced under Hadcho's car. I tried to grab the yellow longhair, but it was skittish. After a couple of attempts to coax it toward me, I gave up. Animal Control would have to lure the cat into a cage.

"That bites," said Hadcho, as he stood at my elbow. He watched the techs struggle to load Marla into the bus. "There wasn't even enough of a pathway through the house for them to use the gurney. Good thing she doesn't weigh much."

"Think she'll make it?"

"Who knows?" Hadcho shrugged. "She wouldn't have a

chance if you two hadn't shown up. That's one lucky scrapbooker."

"Or one unlucky scrapbooker." The revolving red lights of the ambulance bounced off the glass window in Marla's front door.

"Okay," Hadcho grunted. "Let's go over what happened one more time. Take it from the top."

CHAPTER 8

"How come you're here and not at your store?" Hadcho asked.

"Rebekkah." Clancy and I spoke like a Greek chorus.

"Pardon? Is there someone else here?"

"Nope. She's back at the scrapbook store." I hitched my thumb in the general direction of Time in a Bottle. "See, she's Dodie Goldfader's daughter and she's been running the business."

"That's exactly the problem," said Clancy. "Rebekkah shouldn't be running the shop. She doesn't have any experience. But Dodie is the owner, and Rebekkah is her child. We're all dancing *hava negila* to her klezmer band."

"Anyway, Rebekkah came up with this idea to establish community," I explained. "She decided we should sponsor a series of roving scrapbook crops. A crop is basically a scrapbook party. Rebekkah thought we should go from one customer's house to the next. I've been telling Dodie it's a bad idea. It puts too much pressure on people."

"This Mrs. Lever was one of your customers, and you planned to have one of these parties here? That would have been some picnic."

"I had no idea this place was such a mess. You'd never guess it from the address, would you? Marla Lever is a very nice person. Very sweet. She sort of wandered in one day. Then she brought pictures of her cats and wanted to make an album. Next thing I know, Rebekkah says Marla should be our hostess one week."

Hadcho snorted with laughter.

"It gets worse. Rebekkah insisted that Marla should have the other scrapbookers come here. Marla was panicked by the idea, but Rebekkah—"

"We've been saying 'but Rebekkah' a lot lately," Clancy interrupted me.

"But Rebekkah wouldn't let it go. Even when Marla said it wouldn't work for her. Rebekkah kept hounding the poor woman. Finally, Marla said yes. She said that she'd been meaning to tidy up, and this would give her a good excuse."

"Evidently not enough of one," muttered Clancy.

"Since Marla said she needed to tidy up, and because she seemed so reluctant to have the crop here, I suggested that Clancy and I could come early. I figured we could do a quickie cleaning job or help get things ready. I talked to Marla yesterday; she knew what time we were coming. In fact, she said she was trying to get someone to mow her lawn. As you can see that didn't happen."

"Mowing won't cut it." He snickered at his own pun. "Someone needs to spray everything with RoundUp, kill it, and start over."

"As soon as I saw the place, my gut told me there was a problem," I said.

"No kidding?" Hadcho grinned. "What was your first clue, Sherlock?"

I ignored him and kept on talking. "I called Rebekkah while we were sitting in Clancy's car. Of course, she told me she didn't have time to listen to my whining." I did not add that Rebekkah never listened to any of us about anything. She pretty much did as she pleased.

"Kiki's been complaining—" Clancy started.

"Not complaining. Just protesting. Want to make that perfectly clear."

"Protesting, complaining, whatever. Kiki's been telling our boss to re-think this. In fact, Kiki's been worried about Rebekkah's attitude for months." Clancy ended her tirade with a tiny huff of disapproval.

"No joke?" Detective Stan Hadcho pointed his pen at me. "Listen up, Mrs. Lowenstein. Next time you get that ucky feeling, do not pass go. Turn around. Hop in the car. Drive off into the sunset. Got it?"

"What difference does it make?" I shrugged. "Sooner or later somebody had to stumble in on this mess."

"Next time let someone else do the stumbling. Preferably someone with a background in law enforcement. You steer clear of messes."

"Whatever."

"Do you realize how lucky you two were that she's out of it? Mrs. Lever, I mean," Hadcho said. "Things could have been worse for you. Both of you. A lot worse."

CHAPTER 9

"Excuse me?" I had no idea what he meant. Clancy looked puzzled, too.

"This woman is clearly emotionally disturbed," said Hadcho. "Might even have a touch of dementia. Plus she's a hoarder, and what she's doing here breaks the law."

An Animal Control officer dressed in dark brown pants and a neatly pressed khaki shirt waved to Hadcho. "The van's full. We're taking these to the shelter. Another van is on the way."

"Marla's in trouble?" I didn't want that. I was just trying to help. "These cats are her life. You should see the cute album I helped her make with photos of them."

"That's right," said Clancy. "It's the cat's meow."

We all groaned.

"The St. Louis County Ordinance allows homeowners to have five pets," Hadcho said. "Four of any one species. These cats have to go. Once Animal Control gets them all in carriers, they'll take every one of them to the animal shelter. We are lucky, in a way, that Mrs. Lever is out of it. Hoarders do not like seeing their pets taken away. They get militant. Your friend is likely to become un-glued." He laughed and elbowed me. "Get it? A scrapbooker coming unglued?"

That wasn't funny. Not to me.

"Sometimes they go from unglued to violent." Hadcho snapped his fingers. "Like that."

"But they'll take good care of the cats at the animal shelter. They'll find them homes, right? It's a no-kill shelter, so they have to." Even as I said it, I knew better. I felt sick, not sick-at-my-stomach sick like Clancy had been. Sick-at-my-heart sick.

"No, they'll probably put a quarter of them down."

"Put them down? What? Why?"

"Most of them are beyond help. I doubt any of them are up to date on their vaccinations. See that one, over there in the corner? Notice how he's so lethargic? Doesn't even notice his pals being all stirred up. I bet he has feline distemper virus. If one has it, they all probably do. These cats have been sick a long time. See how scrawny that one is? And that one? His eyes are matted shut? And that big black cat in the corner? Notice how dull his coat is? That's one sign of feline leukemia. The vet at the shelter will check them over, but I can tell you from experience that a good number of them will be euthanized," Hadcho said while watching me to see if the horror sunk in.

"That's...awful."

"It's inhumane. Your pal will probably go bonkers when she finds out. You are lucky she was out like a light."

"Yeah," I said. "That's me. I'm really, really lucky."

CHAPTER 10

"Rebekkah?" I held my phone to my ear as I stared out the window into the backyards of neighboring houses. Nice houses. Houses with normal numbers of pets, like two. Upper limit, three. "I need you to call everyone who said she was coming to the crop at Marla Lever's place in Ladue. Tell all our guests the event has been cancelled. Hello? Rebekkah? You there? Could you turn down the music?"

"Can't hear you."

Of course she couldn't. She regularly turned the store radio to the loudest hip-hop station on the dial. This was her little passive aggressive way of protesting the forced change in her lifestyle. Rebekkah recently told her parents that she wasn't sure about her major, accounting. In fact, she wasn't sure she wanted to finish school, period. Her parents said, "No problem. You can think it over in the comfort of our home."

They went back and forth a couple of rounds before Horace rented a Penske van and drove it to the apartment Rebekkah shared with another student. The place was right off the campus of University of Missouri. Rebekkah hadn't come home willingly.

Kicking and screaming are the words that come to mind.

Things got worse. Dodie had discovered a lump in her breast. Horace lost his job. Because he was unemployed, Dodie delayed going to the doctor. She wasn't about to plunge the family into debt for her medical treatment.

Rebekkah had been home three days shen her parents saw the tattoo of St. Francis on her backside—a "tramp stamp" is what they call it. Whatever disagreements the Goldfaders were having about her future escalated into full-blown nuclear warfare.

"You shall not make gashes in your flesh for the dead, or incise any marks on yourselves; I am the Lord." Dodie moaned.

That *thump, thump, thump* sound I heard was her banging her head against her desk. "You've read Leviticus nineteen-twenty-eight! You can't be buried in a Jewish cemetery! Oy!"

"Maybe I don't care!" Rebekkah shouted.

"I'm calling your father. He'll have a heart attack. How could you have ruined your flesh like that! What are you, *meshuggannah*?"

There followed a long, low moan. "Show me. Right now. What is that? Who is that on your *tuches*? Moses Montefiore?"

I pressed my ear against the door. Yes, I know that's rude. I know it was uncalled for. I know it was bad. But I did it. In the interest of research and job security I needed to know what was going on.

"Saint Francis of Assisi."

"Eekkk! You got a tattoo—and it's not even Hebrew? Does it wash off?"

"I hope not. I paid good money for it."

"Argh." This was a gurgle from Dodie.

"Mommy, St. Francis was a good man. He loved animals!"

More moaning.

The door minder dinged, sending me to wait on customers.

Horace Goldfader arrived shortly thereafter. Through the big display window, I watched his car pull into our parking lot. Customers kept me busy after that, except for one time when I raced into the back to check on a special order. Even through the thick walls, I could hear weeping and wailing.

I don't know how they left matters, but shortly after, Dodie printed up business cards identifying Rebekkah as the "Sales Mangler" of Time in a Bottle. I tried not to sit in judgment of the Goldfaders. Being a parent is the hardest job I've ever had, and all of us hire on as amateurs. Had I been in their position, I might have done the same. College wasn't cheap. We certainly needed help at the store. Maybe they reasoned that giving Rebekkah more responsibility would force her to up her game.

"I'd have gotten a tattoo, too, if it meant a promotion," said Clancy when I told her about the family feud that preceded Rebekkah being named Sales Mangler. Clancy and I worked together companionably to trace circles on paper for an upcoming Zentangle® class.

"Not me. No way."

"Prediction." Clancy waved her hands over an imaginary crystal ball. "Big mistake. Big, big mistake. I see a cloudy future, confusion, and many problems ahead for you and me both."

By golly, Clancy had been right.

"And Bama?" I had to throw that in.

"Bama will always come out smelling like a rose." Clancy shook her head. "It's a talent you don't have."

Although Rebekkah was normally a sweetie, her new title had gone straight to her head. And her head was up her butt. Or up her *tuches*, if you prefer the Yiddish word for backside. That meant the title was resting comfortably somewhere between...never mind.

"Is it possible that she's just acting out?" Clancy poured herself a cup of coffee in the back room.

"Acting out?" I didn't get what she meant.

"Yes. Think about it. Dodie finds a lump in her breast. Horace loses his job. Rebekkah decides college is too much for her."

I hadn't seen it that way, but Clancy had a point.

"Horace accepted that job in Chicago. They're working out the details. Or so I've heard."

"Hmmmm. His insurance won't kick in for a while. At least I don't think it will. I'm no expert, but I bet that's why Dodie keeps putting off seeing a doctor."

"Meanwhile, tensions are building." I tried to sound flippant, but my attempt failed.

"You've got that right. There's pressure on Horace to get this wrapped up. Pressure on Dodie because she remembers her mother died of breast cancer, and Rebekkah was far from home. I bet that's one reason she couldn't settle down at college. Too much on her mind."

"You do know that Dodie lost a child, don't you?"

"A son. Nathan." Clancy sighed. "That changes a family's dynamics. I saw it in action when I was a teacher. Not every family acts the same, but I would guess that Nathan's death has made Dodie and Horace more protective of Rebekkah."

"I can't imagine…" and my voice trailed off.

"Neither can I," Clancy agreed.

After that conversation, I felt more compassionate, trying to put myself in Dodie and Horace's place. Why not give their daughter a title? If that encouraged her to be more responsible, a title was a small price to pay.

Except that Dodie and Horace didn't pay the price. Clancy and I did. Day after day, we reaped the bitter harvest from that conciliatory promotion. First we suffered when Rebekkah decided to "build community" by having us travel from home to home. Second, and perhaps more importantly, we got tripped up whenever a problem arose, because Dodie demanded that we take any concerns, questions, or problems directly to Rebekkah. Since I worked the majority of hours on the sales floor and I had the most day-to-day contact with customers, I wound up asking Rebekkah a lot of questions.

Not surprisingly, she came to think of me as a troublemaker. By contrast, Clancy worked so few hours, she rarely had a reason to consult with our Sales Mangler. And Bama? Bama never butted heads with Rebekkah. They seemed to have formed some sort of secret sisterhood, pledging to always see eye-to-eye. Bama could do no wrong.

That left me the odd woman out. Especially when a problem cropped up. A problem like Marla not answering her door.

Rebekkah's way of handling uncomfortable situations was to

take her head out of her butt, stick that same head in the sand, wave her tail feathers in the air, and turn up the volume on her radio. That's exactly what she did when I tried to tell her what was happening with Marla Lever.

"Rebekkah!" I nearly shouted as I stared at the outside world and wished I was free to walk away from this dump. "Listen! There's a problem! You need to—"

My plea was interrupted by a high-pitched screech as Rebekkah switched the phone line to the fax line. Later she would claim it was an accident. I knew she would. But she'd pulled the same trick last week, so I was onto her games.

I hung up on the fax machine and gave Clancy the bad news. "If you've got that checklist, I suppose we could go through the roster and try to call everyone ourselves," I said. "We have a few cell numbers. Most people gave us their email addresses. You could contact them with your Blackberry."

"Will do." Clancy put on her reading glasses. They were by Versace. I put on my reading glasses. Mine were by Walmart. We punched in numbers.

But we weren't fast enough.

The first carload of scrapbookers arrived as we dialed. They parked in front of Marla's house.

"Uh oh." I meant that as code for "rats, dag-nabit" or something stronger.

Four women bailed out of Lottie Feister's car. I could barely see them through the dirty dining room window.

I hopped up from the table where Hadcho was finishing his notes. Even as he yelled at me, I raced to the curb.

"Hi! We're here!" Lottie waved at me. Her smile was as bright and cheery as the orange-red hair she wore on her head.

Clancy tagged along behind me. "Um, Lottie? There's a bit of a problem."

Two more cars showed up. Doors slammed. Three

scrapbookers jumped out of the vehicles, unloading their Cropper-Hoppers and other suitcases on wheels. The women stood on the sidewalk and gaped at the house. Their mouths were hanging so far open that I could count their fillings. They were shocked by the unkempt condition of a building with this expensive address.

"This is Marla's place?" one woman wondered.

"We're having our crop here?" said another.

I stepped in front of the crowd. "Um, everybody? See, I'm very sorry to say, there's a…we have a…"

Clancy grabbed my shoulder and moved me aside. With a crisp clap of her hands, she said, "Listen up! Attention! Marla isn't feeling well. We have to cancel and reschedule."

"Why don't I just drop off this squash casserole? My garden is loaded with squash. In fact, I brought a bag of them, in case anybody wants some." The squash-loving scrapbooker tried to step around Clancy.

"I'd love to relieve you of your squash, but I can't let you inside." I blocked her way. "This might be contagious. You don't want to go in there. Really you don't. You can't."

Another scrapper hoisted a Tupperware cupcake carrier. "I baked all last night so I could ice these this morning. I'll just set them in her kitchen. That's the least I can do."

"No!" I panicked. "That's very nice of you, but Marla's indisposed. Seriously. You can't go in. Not now."

"Marla's indi-what? You mean sick? Is that puke I smell? Over in the bushes?" Casserole woman outflanked me. She moved within two inches of my face and sniffed the air like a beagle.

"Marla's not well. Sorry, there's no help for it. We'll have to reschedule." I stuck a finger inside my collar and pulled it away from my neck, trying to get a little air on my skin.

"If she's sick, we need to go see how we can help." Cupcake Lady turned a high-beam smile on me.

"Somebody else is already here." Lottie pointed to Hadcho's car. Fortunately, it was unmarked. Unfortunately, anyone who knew anything about cop cars would identify it as such. I needed to distract Lottie, pronto.

"Uh, yes, but he's helping Marla. He's a neighbor," I lied, while feeling grateful that the Animal Control Van #1 had left and Van #2 had not yet arrived.

"We could help Marla," said Cupcake Lady.

I closed my eyes and took a deep breath. Any minute uniformed police would be pulling up to assist in closing down Marla's animal hoarding operation. Animal Control officers would be arriving, too. I needed to get these women back in the car and on the road—and I needed to do it quickly.

"Um," I stalled. "That's very kind of you to want to assist. Very kind. But Marla's not doing so hot, and Clancy and I've already been...sick. It's definitely catching. You don't want to get this."

That was true. Marginally true, but true. Encouraged by my own quick thinking, I added, "You'll have to come back another day. We'll reschedule everything."

"I live over on Gravois and drove here all the way from Fenton. Do you know the price of gas? I'm not driving all this way again. I came to scrapbook and I plan to do just that." Lottie crossed her arms over her chest and glared at me.

The other three women mimicked her gesture. Monkey see, monkey do, I guess.

An Animal Control van pulled up as I was talking. Three uniformed Animal Control officers stepped out. Their expressions were grim as they hoisted nets on poles and pet carriers. An SUV from the County Health Department pulled in behind them. These were both followed by a squad car of uniformed officers from Ladue.

"Hey!" said one of the scrappers. "They're going in! All of

them! Let's see what's happening! We can take pictures!"

"Pictures!" squealed the other women. "We love pictures!"

"Whoa! Stop!" Clancy and I threw out our arms in an imitation of school crossing guards. "No!"

Cupcake Lady shoved me to one side. "Move out of my way, Kiki Lowenstein."

"Stop!" I yelled, but the women ran right past me.

A loud Bronx whistle split the air.

Hadcho stomped down the concrete steps, his eyes narrow and angry, his lips twisted into a sneer. One hand rested on his Sam Brown belt and his handcuffs were exposed. His jacket was flipped open and his gun holster gleamed in the hot sun. With that thick black hair of his and his chiseled cheekbones, he could have been Geronimo on the warpath.

"What part of stop don't you understand? Mrs. Lowenstein told you to stop and you didn't listen. Did you? Huh? Ladies, either you back off or you'll be taking pictures in jail. Go away. Pronto. Are we clear? You! You with the cupcakes. Hand them over! Now!"

Cupcake Lady's lower lip quivered, but she did as she was told.

Hadcho snatched them from her and held them at his side. A whiff of chocolate danced in the air.

"These might be evidence," Hadcho said. "Now scat! Go!"

As the women reluctantly headed for their cars, Hadcho beckoned to me and Clancy. "Mrs. Lowenstein? Mrs. Whitehead? Get inside the house. Now."

CHAPTER 11

Later that same afternoon...

While Hadcho worked on his report, I phoned the store again. Fortunately, Rebekkah had disconnected the fax machine. My fingers were crossed that I could talk our Sales Mangler into getting in touch with any stragglers who might have signed up at the last minute to attend our crop. Sometimes people registered online, and I wanted to alert them that the crop had been cancelled.

However, Rebekkah listened long enough to immediately seize on one part of our conversation and one part only: cancelation of an event.

"I can't believe you really canceled the crop!" She was seriously ticked off. "Are you kidding me?"

"You have to understand—" I tried to explain, but Rebekkah cut me off.

"No, *you* have to understand. I'm the manager. If I schedule a crop then you are supposed to hold one!" In my mind's eye, I could see Rebekkah's wild hair, forming a black cloud around her face.

"The police put the kibosh on our happy little gathering," I said. "I had no choice in the matter."

"Yes, but you called the cops, didn't you?" Rebekkah's voice was shrill. "They didn't come out of the blue."

I wanted to defend myself, but then a memory popped into my head, a remembrance of a scene I'd overheard at Starbucks. A woman ordered a decaf, sugar-free, non-fat latte, and the barista called it a "Why Bother?"

That was exactly what we had here, a "Why Bother?" Rebekkah wasn't going to listen or be fair to me. Why waste my time and energy trying to explain what happened at Marla's house?

"Come on back to the store, hear me? You two will have to deal with all the angry customers! I refuse to do it!" yelled Rebekkah into the phone.

Once Hadcho okayed us to leave, we drove immediately back to Time in a Bottle. As we pulled away from Marla's house, I saw a uniformed patrolman plonking down an orange Road Closed cone.

Clancy and I decided to swing through McDonald's and get two large iced teas. We figured we'd lost two quarts of sweat each. Once we were in line, the squawk box asked, "May I take your order?"

We answered by adding two Fillet of Fish sandwiches, fries, and caramel sundaes.

"We deserve it," she said.

"Mmmhmmm." I tried to agree with my mouth full.

Not surprisingly, as soon as we got back to the store, the phone was ringing with disappointed croppers.

Standing at the cash register, I answered the first one, got an earful of complaining, told the scrapbooker I'd call her back later, and realized we needed a game plan. "Clancy? What should we do?"

"First we choose a time to re-schedule. Then we offer them something free to compensate them for their time, money and trouble. We also offer a refund, but the freebie should be cool enough that they refuse the refund and reschedule."

She opened the big datebook that she uses to log all our events. These are also kept in the computer in our Outlook program, but having the datebook at hand means we don't need to boot up the computer to answer a question. Anyway, questions usually occur as people pay for their merchandise when the book is handy.

"What can we offer?" she asked as she stared at the calendar.

"I wish Dodie was here. I'd prefer to get her input."

Clancy's mouth formed a deep frown. "Don't worry about

that. I have a hunch that Dodie will have plenty to say about this. It can all wait until tomorrow. I don't know about you, but I'm wiped out. Exhausted. Emotionally and physically. Between the heat and the mess, I'm beat.

"Me, too," I agreed.

"After work, you have to pick up your daughter, drive home, let out your dog, make dinner, and play mommy. I get to go home to an empty house, take a shower, pour a glass of wine, and hop into bed."

"Sounds heavenly."

Clancy sighed. "It's not. It's just plain pathetic."

CHAPTER 12

Later that evening...

The knock at my front door was unexpected. My daughter and mother-in-law both have their own keys. The visitor was persistent. The noise of bare knuckles against wood rang out over the deep *woof-woof* of my dog, Gracie, a harlequin Great Dane. Most people call Gracie a rescue dog, and that's totally accurate. After my husband George died, Gracie rescued me from despair. I'd always wanted a dog. Seeing poor Gracie squashed into a small metal crate on the sidewalk of a pet shop nearly broke my heart. True, she was an expense I couldn't afford, but one I eagerly took on because I simply couldn't live without her.

"Settle down, Gracie." I hooked a finger under her collar to afford me some control as she pranced in front of the door, willing it to open. That made it nearly impossible for me to get to the peep hole.

"Gracie, move! Let me see who's out there." Shoving her aside takes a bit of muscle because she weighs nearly as much as I do.

Through the hole in the door, I stared into the amazing green eyes of Detective Chad Detweiler, the homicide cop who had worked on my husband's murder case. My heart took a nose dive straight down to my Keds as I yanked the door open.

"So this is your new place." Detweiler's eyes traveled everywhere but seemed to shy away from me.

"Uh-huh." I'd avoided Detweiler for many reasons. Now I could barely bring myself to look at him.

"Better neighborhood."

"Yup." I'd been burglarized at my previous rental home. Home? Hovel is more like it. I'd been living in a dump. I'd found this place with help from my mother-in-law, Sheila, and moved in a month ago.

Detweiler cleared his throat. "Good. Glad you're safe. I came by to see if you're all right. Stan Hadcho called me from the scene. He's my partner, and he knows about your late husband." Detweiler shifted his weight from one foot to the other.

Gracie's cold nose pressed against the back of my leg, causing it to buckle. Or at least, that's my story and I'm sticking to it. Detweiler has this habit of turning me into jelly. I've been keeping my distance from him ever since I discovered he is married. If I needed another reason, his wife had made it clear she knew about me. Staying clear of Detweiler has been hard. Really hard. Our paths seem destined to cross frequently.

He does part-time security for CALA, the Charles and Anne Lindbergh Academy, where Anya goes to school. My new house is on the route he travels from CALA to the police station. Once in a while, I see him drive by, and I've noticed him at school events. I hear about him from his boss, Chief of Police Robbie Holmes, who is dating my mother-in-law, Sheila Lowenstein. For all those reasons and more, our paths occasionally cross, but he has never visited my new place. Not until now.

"Nice house. Good neighborhood." Detweiler repeated himself.

I knew he was wondering how I could afford it. I'd worried about that, too. At first, I doubted I'd ever find a place that satisfied my limited budget, offered an ideal location, and allowed a big dog. Fortunately, bestselling author Leighton Haversham wanted a tenant for his garage-turned-cottage, his failed experiment at writing in a spacious building. He also needed a person who could help him with Petunia, his pug, and Monroe (pronounced Mon-ROW), his donkey. For that he was willing to reduce our rent. The match fit both our needs perfectly.

"I bet Gracie enjoys the big yard."

"She does." In fact, Gracie, Anya, and I all loved the spacious grounds and the huge shade tree. The landscaping was

Leighton's pride and joy, and he had invested hours and dollars into making it spectacular. There was even a small koi pond that Gracie could wade in to cool off on hot summer days.

Throwing her full weight against my legs, the dog pushed past me to get to Detweiler. He squatted down to rub her ears.

"I've missed you." Detweiler bent closer to the dog, but we both knew what he meant. His wife had made a special trip to Time in a Bottle to tell me he missed me and to warn me to stay away from her husband.

I'd done exactly that. Keeping my distance. Ignoring his calls, two letters, and a couple of text messages, but I couldn't deny my intense feelings for the tall, lean detective.

Gracie also had a crush on the cop. My pup loves me, but I have no illusions. In a contest between me and the cop, I'd come in a distant second.

The cool air from my A/C unit rushed past. Even at the end of the day, it was like a blast furnace outside. Usually, I would have slammed the door in a hurry. But how could I when that meant slamming it in Detweiler's face?

As he slowly straightened, I felt torn. "Stan said you walked right into a real mess. Are you okay?"

I nodded. Even though I wanted to forget my visit to Marla Lever's house, I was happy to have a reason to see Detweiler again. Fate had brought us back together...sort of. Seeing him produced a physical ache that no Advil would cure.

"I got to the Lever house an hour after you'd left, and I couldn't believe how bad the place smelled. Must have been a real nightmare when you found your friend lying there on the bed."

"It was. Care to come in where it's cool?" My heart pounded so loudly, I was sure he could hear it. He stepped past me and took a seat on the edge of my sofa. Gracie moved with him, as if she were glued to his side.

"You sure you're all right?" he asked, and the expression on his face was one of real concern.

"Kinda. Sorta."

I tried to wipe the image from my mind, but I'll admit that a part of me was fascinated. How could Marla have lived like that? With all those cats? And the papers? Why wasn't her living room filled sky high with junk, too? Why did no one notice the growing hoard of animals? How had she kept her weird little secret quiet for so long? After all, Marla had smelled of cat urine. Didn't she have any friends who noticed? Did no one try to get her help?

Most intriguing: What would happen next?

"Would you like a glass of iced tea?" I said. Sitting in the same room with him made me antsy.

"Yes, please. Unsweetened."

"Fortunately, I have a lot of ice," I said. "Speaking of which, did you find anything wrong with Marla's A/C?

"The switch had been tripped at her fuse box," said Detweiler. "We didn't find any fingerprints on the toggle. It's weird that no one complained about the smell coming from her house."

"Her place is at the end of the block. It's sort of set apart."

I bustled around in my kitchen. He'd followed me to that room, and now he pulled out a chair and sat down at my table. Although he'd never been in this house before, he seemed to belong. Out of the corner of my eyes, I caught him glancing around and taking the place in.

"Right, but there's a guy who lives behind her. You'd have thought he would have noticed," said the cop. "Of course, people for several blocks over noticed an unusual number of cats wandering around."

"I guess Marla couldn't keep all of them inside. A couple escaped when the EMTs came to take her to the hospital," I said.

"Her lot is pretty secluded. Most of the other residents were happy enough to have a quiet old lady down the street, one who minded her own business. Beats me what they were thinking. Maybe they weren't thinking. We all get busy. Maybe they didn't realize she was accumulating all those cats. Probably a lot of them look somewhat alike."

He continued, "Hadcho told me that Mrs. Lever's daughter and son-in-law stopped by to see her at the hospital. Her son, Allen Lever, showed up, too. Not that they could do much visiting since Mrs. Lever's in a coma. There's not much to charge her with. Animal cruelty. Breaking the city statutes. That's the long and short of it. Unfortunately, Missouri doesn't have any anti-hoarding laws."

"What did her family say?" I handed him his glass before sipping my iced tea and chewing on a mint leaf.

"Her daughter was livid. Went ballistic. I guess they've cleared out Mrs. Lever's house twice before. Mrs. Lever told them she was getting help. Supposedly was on medication. Tofranil? I guess it was prescribed for her years ago, she quit taking it, started up again after her kids begged her. They thought she was getting better. Then this."

"Yeah," I said. "This."

"Ali Lever Timmons threw a tantrum there in the hospital," Detweiler said. "Mrs. Timmons' brother didn't say much. He's a state employee up near Belleville, Illinois. Mr. and Mrs. Timmons live in Illinois, too, just across the river in O'Fallon. I gather the kids and their mother had been estranged, but started talking to Mrs. Lever after she swore she was getting help. They asked if I knew a good cleaning service. I recommended that friend of yours, Mert Chambers. I think she's over there right now to see what she needs. She'll definitely have to rent a Dumpster, and bring in a flock of helpers."

Mert would call me and offer me part-time work. She was my former cleaning lady and my forever best friend. These days I helped her out whenever she had a big cleaning job. I also took in boarders when Mert's petsitting service needed an extra hand. The additional money fed Gracie, bought a few trinkets for Anya, and generally came in handy.

"What happens next? For Marla? I mean after she gets out of the hospital? That is, if she comes out of the coma and can take care of herself?"

"Her house is off limits until they get it cleared and cleaned out," he said. "Mrs. Lever can't go back until it passes inspection.

They were still rounding up cats late this afternoon."

"How many?"

"Eighty-three so far. Five euthanized right away. The vet at the animal shelter will determine whether another dozen can be saved. All were undernourished. Most were sick with mites, mange, feline distemper, worms, and so on. As you know, at least one of them had died recently."

"That's a lot of homeless cats."

"Cats? Did I hear there are cats that need homes?" My daughter Anya walked in on us. She looked a little surprised to see Detweiler, but bless her, she quickly covered her shock.

"Honey, a pet is an expense. We can't afford another animal right now," I said, "besides—"

I didn't have the chance to finish. Detweiler's phone, my phone, and the doorbell all started ringing at once.

CHAPTER 13

. "A corpse? In Marla Lever's deep chest freezer? You mean an animal body, right?" I poured a glass of iced tea for Hadcho, who had shown up at my front door. Of course, I invited him inside and introduced him to Anya. Hadcho joined Detweiler and me at the kitchen table. In short order, both men gulped down their glasses of cold, unsweetened tea, so I put a kettle on the stove to make more.

My hand shook as I brought my own glass to my mouth. Was it really possible that Marla Lever had shared her home with a corpse? A human body seemed unlikely. But another dead cat? Sure. That I could definitely see.

"The corpse is human. Female. We've got ourselves a dead woman," Hadcho said. "When we opened the freezer, the body was there, folded up under packages of ground meat frozen in baggies." He spoke casually, as if he dealt with this every day. But even as he spoke, he kept pinching at the seam of his pants. His handsome features looked drawn and sharp, especially around his high cheekbones.

I cradled my glass in my hands, and stared out the kitchen window at the pen that held Monroe, Leighton's donkey. After Hadcho arrived and took a seat at my table, I had asked my daughter to take Gracie for a short walk around the yard. I also suggested that while she was outside, Anya should check on Monroe's water, since it was so hot. Digging in my chiller drawer, I handed her an apple to feed the donkey.

That chore might keep Anya busy for a half an hour.

My method of diversion wasn't subtle; I'll admit. But Anya didn't need all the gory details of what I mentally labeled "The Marla Lever Case."

"That new patrolman, what's his name?" Hadcho prompted Detweiler. "Lambert? Yes, Lambert, like the airport. He screwed up. I told him to look everywhere. He says he opened the chest, but he didn't rummage around. Didn't look carefully. Saw packages of frozen food and slammed the lid."

"Ugh." I glanced at my own freezer, about the size of a shoebox. No bodies there! No red meat, either. A.) I couldn't afford it. B.) My daughter had become a chick-a-terian. That was our word for "a person who only eats chicken and no other meat."

Since Anya tends to be too thin, I hoped and prayed she would never meet a chicken, close up and personal, so she wouldn't harbor compunctions about having one for dinner. On her plate. Not as a house guest.

Detweiler leaned against my kitchen counter, crossed his long legs at the ankles and sipped his tea. "Ease up, Stan. With all that mess it would be easy to overlook something. Mrs. Lever packed stuff in every nook and cranny. Junk was stacked to the ceiling, too. So Lambert missed something in the freezer. Big deal. You hadn't released the scene."

"No, I hadn't. But I had escorted that cleaning lady—what's her name — through that dump so she could get an idea what she'd be dealing with."

"Mert Chambers." I took the kettle off the stove and poured hot water over tea bags in an old teapot. As an afterthought, I pinched off a stem of mint from the pot in my windowsill. When it hit the water, a fragrance cloud enveloped me. The herb would add flavor and make the drink more cooling to the senses.

"Yes, that's the one," Hadcho said. "The cleaning lady, Mert Chambers. We did a walk through. She asked me if I'd emptied out the freezer. I told her we hadn't, not yet. She made me look inside. Said she didn't want any nasty surprises when she unplugged it. I opened it and shuffled a few packages around. Moved a couple bags of ground meat to one side and found myself staring down at a head full of hair."

"Who was it? I mean, who is the dead person?" I knew I shouldn't ask. In fact, I shouldn't have been included in this conversation at all. As soon as Hadcho came to his senses, he'd realize that. Apparently the heat had gotten to him, too.

"We don't know yet. It's up to the crime scene people. I didn't fish around for an ID because I didn't want to mess up the scene. Better to leave it to the techs. No one would be able to identify that citizen just by looking. Injuries to the face and all."

"Blech." I gagged a little. "Totally gross."

"I forgot that you're a civilian."

A civilian. Right. That was a pretty good definition of my status. I was definitely not cut out for a career in law enforcement.

Detweiler walked over to my kitchen window and checked on Anya. He smiled at me, reading my mind. "She's fine. She's giving Monroe a tummy rub. I can see her from here."

I glanced down at my phone and saw I'd missed a call.

"If you two will excuse me, I'm going to see what Mert needs. Probably wants help cleaning the Lever house."

"Tell your friend thanks a lot for messing up my crime scene," Hadcho said.

That ticked me off. "My friend saved you a lot of grief. She's a professional. She's good at her job. So your flunkie didn't do his. Woop-de-do. Mert did hers."

"What makes you think your pal saved me a lot of grief?" Hadcho wrinkled his brow.

"What if we had unplugged the freezer and didn't get back to it? What if stuff started to defrost? The remains would have been a lot harder to process, wouldn't they?" Over the years, I'd had enough experience with appliances on the blink that I could imagine the mess.

"I suppose that would have been better for Mrs. Lever," grumped Hadcho. "Her house. Her freezer. Her victim."

"Stan, you know that's a leap," said Detweiler in a warning

tone.

"Just because she hoards cats doesn't make her a killer." I poured the freshly brewed tea into a carafe and added ice cubes to the mix.

"Whether she is or isn't," Detweiler said to his partner, "we're lucky Kiki and her pal found the woman. From what I heard, Mrs. Lever and her kids have an on-again off-again type of relationship. Who knows how long it would have taken for someone to report her missing? Another day in this heat and we'd have been stuck with a corpse in the bedroom and a human Popsicle in the freezer. When the power company turned off her electricity—which would have happened eventually—our corpse would have turned to goop."

"I bet goop is hard to identify. Compared to a human Popsicle, that is," I said.

"All right already. So Mrs. Lowenstein and her friend did us a favor. Satisfied? I'll play nicely. But we're spinning our wheels until we get an ID on the body," Hadcho said.

"What's the last report from the hospital? Any word on Mrs. Lever's condition?" Detweiler rinsed his glass out.

"Not good," Hadcho said. "The docs figure it for a stroke, aggravated by heat prostration and dehydration. Something or someone tripped the switch in her fuse box and turned off her A/C."

"Seems pretty convenient." I refreshed the ice in Hadcho's glass and poured him more tea.

"What do you mean?" He thanked me and raised an eyebrow.

"I bet Marla Lever hasn't had visitors in ages. How come her A/C stopped today? When she expected us? I could tell she didn't want us to come, but she didn't flat out say, 'No.' She did tell me she was nervous about getting her lawn mowed. But she didn't say anything about the air conditioning being out, and that would have been first on anyone's list. Especially considering this heat wave and how closed up her place was. And the smell. I mean, it was bound to be bad under any circumstances, but without A/C it was stifling."

Hadcho downed his glass of iced tea in two long gulps. "Remember, we're dealing with a whack-job here. Hoarders are delusional. She probably thinks she's the next Martha Stewart."

"But she was nervous about your visit, right?" Detweiler asked me. "Maybe she was nervous about someone reporting her to Animal Control."

"I don't think so. We all knew she had cats. Lots of them. She brought photos to the store to scrapbook. That's how we met her. Sure, she had a few pictures of her kids, both when they were young and after they'd grown. But only about four of those. Mainly she had pictures of cats. I think for her, the large number of pets was, well, normal. She never mentioned a specific number. What's the pathology of this? Of animal hoarding?"

"There are all sorts of theories," Detweiler said. "Some psychologists think it's a type of OCD. Others say it has aspects of borderline personality disorder and addiction. A new theory suggests it's an attachment disorder. There seems to be a lot of support for hoarding being a delusional disorder. Animal hoarders rationalize away reality. She might have told herself that a large number like that was normal. Or that she was doing them a favor."

"But the timing." I shook my head. "That's what gets me. Why'd this have to happen when we were planning to visit?"

"Because you're lucky," Hadcho said with a grin. "Lucky, lucky, Kiki Lowenstein."

CHAPTER 14

The cops thanked me for the iced tea and then they left, freeing me to call Mert.

"Are you in or out?" she asked.

My friend could be a woman of few words. Mert was one of a kind, a powerhouse of energy, and a pragmatist to the core.

"You bet I'm in. I can use the money. Rebekkah slashed my hours." With the phone tucked under my ear, I rinsed out Gracie's dish, scalded the sink and cleaned my countertops. Anya had showered and gone to bed. I was alone in my kitchen, and free to talk to my BFF candidly.

"That's 'cause you honk Rebekkah off." A slurp told me Mert was drinking a Bud Light, one of her favorite after work treats.

"The feeling is mutual. I used to really, really like that kid, but a little bit of power has gone to her head. When I do go in, she dumps all the grunt work on me. The stuff she doesn't like to do."

Mert chuckled. "What is it that she likes doing?"

"As soon as I figure that out, I'll let you know."

"You do realize this will be an ugly job. But you'll get extra pay." There was a clanking sound as the phone bumped up against the many earrings Mert wore.

"Because it's ugly?"

"No, because we have to wear biohazard suits."

"You are kidding!"

"Nope. With all that cat ca-ca spread all around, we might pick up something nasty. Don't want us breathing that stuff, neither. You know how much it's going to cost 'em to get that house cleaned out?"

"I have no idea."

"Forty grand."

"Wha-what?"

"Yes, ma'am. This is the second time they've had to take the place down to the bare nubbins. You shoulda heard her daughter yelling about it."

"Why not just bulldoze the house?"

"Because Marla Lever owns it, not her kids. If it were up to them, that'd be Ladue's newest teardown."

"But they have neighborhood ordinances, don't they? Most neighborhoods do."

"Yep, but they'd have a go 'round with Marla, she'd get stuff up to snuff, and then let it slide again. At least that's what the daughter said."

"Who's paying for the clean-up?"

"Marla took a second mortgage out on her house a while back.

Her daughter has signing privileges. Get this, Marla's got a quarter of a million bucks in the bank. Her kid said Marla used to have more, through an inheritance, but most of the dough has gone to lawyers. I guess old Marla keeps fighting to keep her animals."

"What's her daughter like?"

"I wouldn't cross a street to say hi to Allison Lever Timmons. She ain't the nicest person I've ever met. She thinks her you-know-what don't stink, probably because she's got a hot-shot job in an investment firm. I think she's an executive secretary. Maybe she was born with her nose stuck up in the air." Mert chuckled. "But, hey, she's under a lot of stress. Her mama keeps collecting animals and junk. Ali keeps getting dragged into it. She's the one authorities call and complain to, 'cause her momma won't listen. The time before this it was birds. Parrots, finches, crows, canaries, wild birds that shouldn't have been kept in cages. They was flying all over and pooping wherever they wished. Before that, old Marla collected fish. But they all died when the power went out. Stunk to high heavens. Can you imagine?"

I had sympathy for Ali Lever Timmons. "I don't want to imagine it. There's nothing she can do?"

"What? Commit her mother? For what? For hoarding? I don't think that goose would fly."

I got off the phone feeling raw and unsettled. After brewing myself a cup of chamomile tea, I sank down on my sofa and reviewed what I knew about Marla. I cast my mind back to the day we'd met.

CHAPTER 15

Six months prior...

The big Valentine's Day rush was over, and the shelves at Time in a Bottle needed restocking. I carried a basket full of new papers to put on our racks. Usually this was a task that fell to Bama Vess, Dodie's other employee, but Bama and her sister had gone on a vacation. They'd rented a cabin in the Ozarks.

I wished I had the money to do something similar.

The door minder rang and in wandered a woman who immediately brought one word to mind: Gray. Her complexion was murky, and her face was closed under a cloud of frizzy gray hair. On her feet were worn and dirty tennis shoes. The hem of a dingy white blouse hung crookedly from under a plastic see-through rain coat. A thick but grubby fisherman sweater drooped on her, the sloppy size visible through the plastic. Over one arm she carried a tired purse that once had been the color of cement. Her pants had faded to a shade between black and old iron.

"Welcome. May I help you find something?" I asked in my best yippee-skippee voice. Early on, I decided that I would treat every customer like visiting royalty. Living is hard and judging is easy.

"Looking," she said, dropping the word "just."

"Enjoy. There's so much to see. Our customers' projects are on the clothesline strung around the top of the walls. We also have displays on top of the shelving units."

She nodded and followed my pointer finger upwards. With her head tilted back, Marla stared at the page displays that ran the perimeter of our store. As her eyes made progress, she did a slow shuffle, moving in a circle. "Those are really something!"

"Don't forget to check out the top of the display shelves."

Marla shifted her gaze so she could take in the pages I'd created and mounted on foam core board. When she got to the display for a new class called "My Life Highlights," she moved closer for a better view. "My, my," she said. "Pets! Animals! I thought scrapbookers only took photos of their families."

"Aren't your pets part of your family?"

"Family," said Marla. "My babies."

"That's how I feel about my pets, too. I love all sorts of animals." With that I reached under my work table to withdraw a small album labeled "Critters." Inside were pictures of the box turtles that had once been such frequent travelers on our roads, but were now scarce. I also had a photo of a blue-lined skink who had lived in our woodpile in Ladue, a pair of squirrels who raced up and down our maple tree, a bullfrog that Anya caught in a local pond (and released!), crawdads that her pre-school class caught, a turtle sunning itself on a branch sticking out of the pond at St. Albans, and one of my favorites, a family of skunks.

"As you can see, I'm really into animals. So is my daughter. See the skunks? My daughter and I were on Wildhorse Creek Road, near St. Albans, when they crawled out from under a drain pipe. I stopped the car to let that mama and her babies cross the street. My daughter went nuts. She wanted to take them home. If I hadn't hit the door lock button, she'd have gone after them, for sure."

"Cats?" Marla asked. "I'd like pictures of my cats. In an album."

"Then you've come to the right place."

Marla's smile lit up her face.

I told Marla our special sessions for beginners might be a good place to start. We call them "Newbie Do-bie Do" classes.

"I can do this?" She gestured to the rows of pages we displayed on our walls.

"Absolutely. I'll teach you how."

"I'll think about it." She hesitated. "I've got money, you know."

I didn't know. I figured we'd work something out if she didn't. A few days later she returned and pulled a wad of photos from a dingy cloth purse. "Where do I sign up for your class?"

I added her to the roster. We looked over her photos together.

Viewing other people's pictures is definitely one of the best parts of my job. Marla pointed out her children, talked about them briefly, and then pushed those photos aside quickly. She grew animated when she came to the pictures of her cats, telling me their names and describing their personalities in great detail. At long last, we came to photos of a little boy, taken by an old Polaroid Swinger Camera. These she touched with a sort of reverence.

"Anthony Dale Lever. Died when he was seven. Fell off a swing. Messing around. Showing off. Like kids do. Took him to the playground and I…my back was turned." Her voice cracked a little. "I should have protected my baby."

My mouth went dry as we both considered every parent's greatest fear, the loss of a child. I couldn't imagine life without Anya.

As always, the only suitable response to so much emotion was to offer our guest a cold beverage from the refrigerator in the backroom. The trip from the front of the store to the stockroom would give her a bit of privacy and give me a chance to get control of myself. I snapped up a Diet Dr Pepper for me and a cold Coke for Marla.

But when I returned to the sales floor, Marla had vanished.

CHAPTER 16

Present day...

Since the day she was born, Anya had been my first and last waking thought. I ended every day by checking on my daughter, reassuring myself she was fine. Tonight Anya was asleep in her bed, curled on one side. Gracie rested on an old braided rug at the foot of Anya's bed.

If only I could keep her from every pain and heartache that life would send my daughter's way!

If only.

Since my husband George's murder, I'd come to realize that the world is a messy and unpredictable place. People you trust can deceive you. Even when they love you, people can let you down.

Marla had let her son Anthony down. Clearly, she'd never forgiven herself or gotten over his death. How could she? How could any mother?

Perhaps Marla's cats were a source of comfort when she lost her son.

I couldn't imagine the sort of damage a person's psyche would sustain when forced to endure the loss of a child. Correction: I didn't want to imagine the pain.

Feeling restless, I searched my kitchen cabinets until I found a small white candle. I lit it and said a prayer. I asked God to watch over Marla. And of course, I asked him to bless my daughter.

The next morning, I woke up with a bad headache. Fighting the pain, I grabbed a bag of coffee the wrong way, and the last of the precious beans dumped all over my kitchen floor. I'm not a germ-o-phobe; I swept up the brown beans, intending to use them. On closer examination, I had also gathered a nice clump of dog hair. I tried to pick the hairs out, but that didn't work. Maybe

I could blow away the hairs, the way my mother used to blow away the spent birdseed in our parakeet's cage. That helped a little, but not enough.

Should I give in and put the beans in the grinder? The hairs would count as fiber.

Even with my incredibly low standards, I couldn't do it. I would have to forego coffee. Given my headache, I saw no relief from feeling foggy and dull.

Food would help. I poured milk over my generic cereal and a clog of white goop fell into the bowl. I stared at it. What on earth? I stood there, trying to decide if the milk was frozen or if it had turned to cottage cheese.

Gracie sniffed the air.

"I have a bad feeling about this," I told her. "Looks like I need to dip a finger in that white mess and taste it. Ugh. Definitely not good. Totally inedible."

"Nuts," I said. But I didn't have any. The cupboard was bare.

Gracie pricked up her ears. A knock on the backdoor followed. The sound signaled the arrival of my neighbor and landlord, Leighton Haversham. I hesitated because I wasn't appropriately dressed for company, but Leighton knocked again.

"This'll have to do," I told Gracie as I looked down at my extra-long tee-shirt. "I'm gorgeous and I know it," was printed across my chest. The shirt had been a gag gift from Mert. Since I still had eye-ookies stuck to my lashes, and my hair stuck out like I'd stuck my finger in a light socket, the slogan seemed comical. But for the most part I was fully dressed. Sort of.

"Hi." Leighton smiled at me. He took in my weird attire and apologized. "Sorry if I woke you up. Did you remember that I'm leaving this morning for a book tour?"

"I remember. I'm just moving slowly. I'm taking care of Petunia and Monroe while you're gone."

"Right." In Leighton's arms he held Petunia, a neutered male pug who stared at me with goo-goo-googly eyes. My landlord delivered the pup to me. Tunie wriggled into a new position so he could lick my face. I responded by blinking and trying to focus. But I was largely unsuccessful. Leighton wore a puzzled expression, as if trying to figure me out.

"You need coffee."

"I sure do. I spilled the beans. Uh, my beans. The coffee beans. Uh, you wouldn't happen to have any lying around?"

"Sure do. Anything else you need?"

"Milk? Cereal?"

"Be right back."

Five minutes later, he handed over a fabric shopping sack with a new bag of freshly ground Columbian coffee, a half-gallon of milk, and two boxes of high quality granola. "How much do I owe you?" I asked.

"Not a cent. You look like you need this more than I do. It would have all gone bad before I got back. Have a good day."

Things were looking up, but I was still running behind, and the Universe decided not to cooperate with me. I discovered a rip in my favorite knit top, right along the seam. Anya wouldn't get out of the shower. Gracie and Petunia decided to sniff every inch of grass between the house and my car before emptying their bladders. Anya stood beside my old BMW and she wore a daydreaming sort of look on her face. First I loaded Petunia into the backseat. Then I urged Gracie to climb in. She was half in and half out when she spotted the squirrel.

My gosh.

There's this one squirrel in our backyard who seems to know how to tease Gracie. That rodent races toward my dog and darts away, over and over. To Gracie, this behavior is like waving the green flag at a race car driver in the Indy 500. Her motor revs into high gear— and she's off.

On this particular morning, my Great Dane nearly yanked my arm out of the socket. Since my dog and I weigh roughly the same, it's a real tussle to get her under control. Today, she took full advantage of the surprise. I still had one hand tucked under her collar when she took off. I followed along as she leaped toward the nearest oak tree. I took two stumbling steps forward before catching my toe under a root. That brought me down face first into the dirt.

"Anya! Help me! Grab her."

Anya took off after Gracie and caught the dog. From my spot on the ground, I watched my daughter clip the leash onto Gracie's collar while I picked bits of grass out of my teeth.

What a start to the day.

CHAPTER 17

I dropped Anya off at the St. Louis Science Center, where she reluctantly climbed out of the car. "I'm not a baby, and I hate summer camp," she said before slamming the door on my old BMW.

"Have a nice day!" I called to her retreating back. "Your grandmother will pick you up."

Anya lifted one shoulder in a half-hearted signal before I drove off.

I like getting to work at least an hour before the store opens. However, on this particular morning I counted myself lucky to slip in with five minutes to spare. Gracie and Petunia went into the doggy playpen obediently. I put away my purse and my lunchbox. After snapping on the lights, I walked to the front door and flipped the sign from CLOSED to OPEN.

I had opened our money drawer and was getting set up for the day when the back door slammed. Rebekkah came strolling in, fifteen minutes late. She looked around, saw that I was at the checkout counter and turned to go back into her mother's office.

"You remembered to stop by the bank?" I called after her.

"I forgot." She kept walking.

That left us with only two ten dollar bills and a roll of pennies. While it's becoming less and less frequent that our scrapbookers pay with cash, we typically keep two twenties, three tens, four fives, twenty ones, and an assortment of quarters, nickels, and dimes in the cash register. As it stood, we wouldn't be able to make change for a twenty or a ten, the two bills most frequently presented.

This did not make me happy.

Behind the cash register was the reservation tally, a list showing me how many people had signed up to attend that evening's crop. There were no names on the list. That didn't make any sense.

We always have a full house for our Friday crops. Always.

"Rebekkah?" I stuck my head inside the office. The Sales Mangler was sitting in her mother's chair, reading a copy of Rolling Stone Magazine. "Do you know how many people are coming tonight?"

"Nope."

I took a deep breath. "We usually keep a reservation tally. Have you been recording names somewhere else?"

She squinted at me. "Isn't that your job?"

I counted to ten. "Not if they call when I'm not here. Or if they send an RSVP by email."

"I'd say plan for the usual number. I didn't have time to write down all the names. I was busy when they called."

"If I don't have a list of names, how am I supposed to know how many kits we need? Or did you already put the kits together? You were going to kit stuff up while I was running the crop at Marla's, right?"

She examined a fingernail very, very closely. "Like I said, I got busy."

"What exactly does that mean? Busy? Did you do some other chore I'm not familiar with?"

She reached into the top drawer of the desk and found her iPod. With a deft move, she stuck the ear buds into her ears before turning to me and saying, "That means, I think I told Clancy to take care of the kits. Maybe. Now go away. Like I told you, I'm busy."

She was busy?

I was so angry I could have spit thumbtacks.

While I stood there fuming, she ignored me and sang, "Want your body, love your body." That made me see red, literally. Another minute and I would start screaming. Instead, I turned on my heel and left the office. Once I made it to the sales floor, I went directly to my work table. Underneath was the plastic storage container where we keep the "make-and-take" kits for each upcoming event.

Nothing was there. Nothing. Not one blessed kit.

I stood there seething.

The phone rang. I moved over to the checkout stand to grab it. My hand was on the receiver when I recognized Dodie and Horace's home number, so I didn't pick up. Instead, I turned away and walked back toward the office. Before I got there, I heard Rebekkah yelling, "Not my fault! Talk to Kiki! She's the one who called it off! Kiki!"

Rebekkah stepped outside the office. "Kiki? Mom wants to talk to you!"

"I'll take it up front."

"Lottie Feister called." Dodie sounded irked from the other end of the phone.

"I just bet she did."

"She wasn't happy."

"No, I imagine not."

"Why did you cancel that crop? You know that means lost income. We'll have a hoard of angry scrapbookers wanting refunds and discounts. You have no authority to cancel crops! I'm the big kahuna, and Rebekkah is the store manager. It should have been her decision."

"I wish it had been. I wish she would take responsibility for something. Anything! Your daughter knows exactly why the crop was canceled. Frankly, I'm surprised she didn't tell you. Clancy called her from the Lever house. We found Marla unconscious in her bedroom. The temp inside the house was in the mid-90s, and guess what? Marla's a hoarder, so there were stacks and stacks of newspaper in the place. Just an itty bitty path to walk along. There were also nearly a hundred cats. And no litter boxes. Instead, they used every available surface. You can guess how the place stunk."

"What?" Dodie choked out the word.

"It gets better. Did you hear about the dead cat in the middle of Marla's dining room table? Hmm? Or the herds of starving kitties who crawled all over us? Huh? Personally, I think those were great reasons for canceling the event. And there's more," I took a deep breath because now I was practically screaming into the phone, "Yes, more, Dodie. It got worse. You see I sent everyone packing before the police found the dead human being in the freezer. Uh-huh, you heard me. The cops found a corpse with a bashed in face. Consequently, I don't much care if Lottie Feister is calling you and complaining. Nope. I'm happy she's calling and complaining. Because she doesn't have much to complain about!"

"I-I-I—" Dodie stuttered. "I didn't know—"

"No, you didn't know and you didn't ask. You didn't give me the benefit of the doubt, did you? You didn't stop to think that I was the last person who'd want to miss out on extra income. So, yes, I canceled the crop. And yes, I'll call everyone and grovel. I was already planning to offer coupons and a make-up session. But here's the deal: I just hope that no one took any pictures, because the scene at Marla's wasn't something I particularly want to put on a scrapbook page. But hey, what do I know? Rebekkah's our hotshot expert. Maybe she'll want to schedule our next outing at the morgue!"

"Now, Kiki —" Dodie shifted into conciliatory mode.

"Don't you 'now, Kiki' me. Do you realize that we have a crop tonight and your daughter hasn't made a list of attendees? We don't have any kits made up, because she didn't do them. Worse luck, I have no idea how many people to plan for. Maybe I should just take the night off and leave this mess to our Sales Mangler!"

With that I banged down the phone.

CHAPTER 18

Rebekkah must have been listening to my tirade, because the minute I was off the phone, she turned up her music full blast.

Rather than make the situation worse, I decided to steer clear of S & M, aka the Sales Mangler. I needed to simmer down.

First I would tidy the shelves and then I planned to restock merchandise, before starting on the prep for the evening's event. Of course, I'd no more than gotten started on these chores when Lottie Feister walked through the door.

"Lottie, I want to apologize for any inconvenience that we caused you yesterday. Here, let me give you a gift certificate. It's not much, but it's our way of saying we feel bad for your trouble." I moved quickly to my work table and I didn't look up as I fumbled for the certificate.

A hand grabbed mine. "Nonsense. I heard about it on the late-late news. A dead body? In the freezer? You will tell me all the details, won't you, Kiki? I mean, you owe me that much. Were there really nearly a hundred cats? And the newspapers. Were they really stacked from floor to ceiling?" Lottie patted her hair into place, an unnecessary gesture since it was sprayed stiff and hard as a beetle's shell. "All my friends called me and wanted to hear what I saw. I have three lunch dates and one invitation to dinner this week alone. I guess they're banking on me telling them more about that house—and the horrible conditions inside."

Her eyes sought mine eagerly.

Lottie had always struck me as a lonely woman, a person who didn't get out much. Her excitement confirmed my suspicions. All she wanted was a bit of attention. A chance to feel important. Didn't we all want the same? To be noticed? To feel like we were special?

I shouldn't have been surprised about Lottie's about-face.

Hoarders had become "sexy," now that they'd been featured

on Animal Planet. Out of the closet and into the light of day, so to speak.

"Lottie, you know nearly as much as I do. You saw the condition of the property."

"Yes, but you went inside! What did it look like?"

"Lots of cats and lots of newspaper."

"Huh? Could you repeat that?"

"Cats and newspapers." I raised my voice.

"I'm talking about the dead body. Did you see that?"

"No," I answered. "I didn't."

She tried a couple more times to get me to elaborate. Finally, I said, "Hey, Lottie, why don't I show you the new paper we got in from K & Co.? We haven't even put it on the floor yet. You'll be the first to play with it. I'm teaching a class in Zentangle®. Can I show some of my tangles to you?"

"All right, but you'll have to talk up. I can hardly hear you over that racket."

"That racket" was Rebekkah's music. I stuck my head in Dodie's office and asked Rebekkah to dial it down a notch. "Our customer says she can't hear me."

Rebekkah grumped, but did as I requested.

"Zen-what?" asked Lottie as I took a spot next to her on the work table.

"Zentangle. It's an art form built on repetitive patterns. Let me show you."

There's nothing scrapbookers like better than new techniques. Although some might not immediately see Zentangle as a scrapbook technique, there are certainly ways to use it to decorate scrapbook pages. As an additional benefit, "tangling" or doing a Zentangle pattern calms the mind. There's something distinctly meditative about the repetitive motion. I've found that once I commit myself to the process I recognize a distinct "click" as my brain shifts from overactive mode to calm and centered. Sure, that didn't happen overnight, but it's now a process I can rely upon. A process that Lottie would enjoy.

"You did all this? By hand?" Lottie stared at the portfolio of Zentangle tiles.

"Yes," I said proudly.

She shook her head. "I could never learn to do that."

"Of course you can. Come over here and sit down. I'll get you started."

I was teaching Lottie a complicated tangle, or Zentangle design, when Dodie walked in.

CHAPTER 19

Dodie walked over to where Lottie and I were working. As usual, my boss clumped along, her feet hitting the floor heavily. Dodie Goldfader was a large woman and a hairy one as well. Years ago, a customer had teased that she was the original wooly mammoth. But under that furry exterior was an elegant mind and a generous heart. After my husband died, Dodie guided me into adulthood by reminding me that I was a single mother with a dependent, so I could no longer afford to turn a blind eye to my finances. She offered me a job here in her store where I'd been her best customer. It was my first real job ever, besides babysitting while I was growing up.

For the most part, Dodie was a terrific boss. Despite the fact that this was a small shop, Dodie always encouraged me to put Anya first, even if it meant closing the doors while I raced to my daughter's aid. "Family first," she always said. "If you aren't happy, you can't make our customers happy and my bottom line will suffer." Yes, Dodie had certainly taught me a lot about being a businessperson.

Really, I owed her a lot. She'd been a wonderful friend and mentor. I hated that she was mad at me.

After saying hello to Lottie, my boss greeted me with, "Hello, Sunshine."

I breathed the proverbial sigh of relief. I'd been afraid that Dodie would be angry, but she didn't seem at all upset. At least, not with me. She peered over Lottie's shoulder and smiled with approval at the Zentangle our customer had created. "Lottie, you are good at that! That is beautiful!"

Dodie knew how to make customers happy. That was one of her secrets of success. She also knew how to merchandise, how to get discounts from manufacturers, how to create customer loyalty, and how to hire good people. But this adventure with her daughter, well, it wasn't her finest moment.

Lottie held up her project for further inspection and broke into a sunbeam grin. "I think I am good at this! I can't wait to see how this will look on a page. Isn't it just the cutest frame? I plan to put a photo inside it. I can keep the pen and the tiles in my purse. It'll give me something to do while I'm at the doctor's office. My hubby, Gene, has pancreatic cancer, you see. He's been in the hospital all week. We're hoping he'll be strong enough to leave soon. Then he'll start chemo and radiation."

Dodie put a gentle hand on the other woman's shoulder. "I know this has been a hard time for you."

I bit my lip rather than blurt out, "See, Dodie? You have to catch these things early." When I collected myself, I stammered, "I'm sorry, Lottie, you must have a lot on your plate."

There it was, the bald truth. You could judge and judge someone, but you never knew what they were coping with. When you learned their situation, you hated yourself for being so hasty. Lord knows, I try to be a better person, but each time I vow to improve, I stumble again. Poor Lottie, she only wanted a distraction—and Marla Lever had provided it.

"Kiki, may I talk with you?" Dodie jerked her head toward the stockroom.

"I'll be right back, Lottie. Would you like a Diet Dr Pepper or a Coke?"

"Love a regular Coke."

"I'll get you one," I said as I padded after Dodie. The minute the stockroom door closed behind us, we both realized we couldn't talk over the loud music Rebekkah was playing. Dodie used a nod of her head to suggest that we step outside the back door.

"I apolo —" I started, but Dodie interrupted me with, "Rebekkah is driving her dad and me *meshugenah*."

"Your daughter doesn't want to be here."

"I know." The dark circles under Dodie's eyes had grown bigger since Rebekkah moved back in with her parents. Or was it a sign that Dodie's health had further deteriorated? "My daughter doesn't know what she wants and she's taking it out on all of us."

"Let's not worry about that now," I suggested. "Lottie's fine, as you can see. She was put out yesterday, and I can't blame her. But there was nothing we could do. Dodie, you have no idea how bad that house stunk or the mess we found."

"I should have listened to you."

Blow me down, Popeye. That's as close to an apology as I've ever heard from Dodie. She's great about a lot of things, but apologizing? You might as well wait for the Sahara to freeze over. I blinked in surprise.

"Let's discuss it later," I said. "I'll come up with a way to make our customers happy despite the inconvenience."

"I know you will. I can always count on you, Kiki."

That put a lump in my throat, so I was grateful for the chance to swing by the refrigerator and grab two colas—one for Lottie and one for me—as I made my way through the stockroom. As I stood in front of the big white GE appliance, I paused to sniff the wonderful aroma of a Frito Pie Casserole. Dodie must have brought it in. My mouth started watering.

Suddenly, I found myself looking forward to our Friday Night Crop.

CHAPTER 20

After she downed the Coke, Lottie became more talkative. Turns out, she and Marla had chatted with each other at the store.

Somehow I'd missed that. Entirely. I don't know where I was when it happened.

"Marla seemed to keep to herself," I said. "I didn't know she talked to anyone!"

"She's shy," said Lottie, "but one of her cats is a Manx, and I used to have a Manx, so we struck up a conversation. Of course, I had no idea she owned so many animals. It never occurred to me that she had a house full. I told her I had a couple dozen cans of cat food left over from Rollo, so I gave them to Marla. She was grateful. Now I know why."

"Feeding Gracie is an expensive proposition, and that's only one dog, albeit a big one. I can't imagine feeding all those cats."

"Her neighbor helped," said Lottie.

"Which one?"

"That guy who lives directly behind her. The one with the nice lawn and all the plants. She told me."

"Good to hear about neighbors reaching out to each other. Again, I'm so sorry for the inconvenience," I said. "You are welcome to come to the crop tonight as my special guest."

"Will there be food?"

"Isn't there always?" I said.

"Count me in."

That was settled. Now all I needed was to come up with a quick "make-and-take" idea. I needed something fast, cheap, and simple because I didn't have time to "kit up" a complicated project. Most of the time, we make money on our crops because I keep the costs low. I do that by "kitting up" the items we use for each project. Instead of giving each scrapbooker an entire sheet of paper, when they only need a small square, we cut the paper into small squares to spread out the cost.

"Dodie? I need to come up with a crop project." I stuck my head inside the door of her office. Rebekkah slipped past me. I heard the back door slam behind her. I knew exactly why she had escaped in such a hurry.

"Excuse me?" Dodie looked up from her paperwork.

"Here's the original kit and the original instructions." I tossed the packets onto Dodie's desk. "But as I told you on the phone, Rebekkah didn't put together the kits. We don't have a good number for our attendees. I could try throwing something together, but I have no idea how many to make. Plus, I don't really have time to cut all the small pieces, so these kits would be more expensive than most. Since I don't have an exact number, I'm likely to create too many kits or too few."

Dodie's mouth settled into a sour frown. "Do what you have to do."

"Let me take Gracie and Petunia for a stroll around the block. I need the fresh air. They need a potty break, and maybe I'll come up with an idea."

Dodie waved me away. The expression on her face was one of pure disgust, but I knew she wasn't mad at me. She'd put us in this tough situation, and now she was reaping the rewards. Or whatever.

Gracie dutifully walked beside me as we circled our block. Petunia zigzagged along, raising his leg at every vertical object.

Time in a Bottle is located smack-dab in the middle of the metro-St. Louis area, which makes us a favorite for papercrafters. But the neighborhood around us can best be described as "transitional." Residences bump shoulders with small businesses like ours. Someday, this will all be retail space. Dodie and her husband Horace had been smart enough to snap up a distressed building, a former auto parts store, five years ago. While their remodeling efforts were not extensive, they'd done enough to make the store a pleasant spot for our shoppers.

Petunia's antics distracted Gracie and she didn't do her business. I extended our walk, leading the dogs to the next block over. A drycleaner sat on the corner, next to a small social services agency, and finally a tiny restaurant, a soup kitchen. The sign noted that the place had been sold and would be changing management. The thought of a nice neighborhood place to have a hot meal pleased me. I hoped the food would be passable and the prices would be reasonable. When my dogs and I rounded the corner, the Great Dane found the perfect spot to squat. The heat pressed on us, growing more and more bothersome by the minute. Trickles of perspiration ran down my back.

Instead of taking the long way around that second block, I decided we should cut through the alley. As we did, our path took us past the now vacant restaurant. Evidently the real estate agent had done a bit of cleaning to make the place presentable because black garbage bags overflowed with empty cans. One, an empty container of pork and beans, had rolled out into the alley. Gracie and I stepped over it, and Petunia skirted it, on our journey back to Time in a Bottle. But the thought of leaving the can in the middle of the pathway disturbed me. I picked it up with the intention of putting it in the recycling bin at the store.

"Come up with an idea?" Dodie called to me as I locked Gracie and Petunia in the doggy playpen.

"Nope," I said.

"What's with the tin can? You panhandling?"

"Not yet." I stared down at the container in my hand. "This was sitting out there in the street. You know how I hate littering. I thought I'd bring it here and..."

An idea struck me hard and shook me like I was an oak tree in a lightning storm. "I've got it! Be right back!"

In five minutes, I was back with two garbage bags full of cans. I filled two buckets with hot water and proceeded to soak off the labels. Dodie came over to watch.

"I'd help you but I don't know what you're doing," she said.

"Help me clean these and soak off the labels. But be careful not to cut yourself."

As we worked peeling off the paper, I asked, "Do we still have those big rolls of brown wrapping paper? The kraft paper?"

"Yes."

"Great!"

"Why do you want kraft paper when we sell scrapbook paper?"

"Kraft paper is different texture," I explained. "It's much tougher and more tear resistant."

"So?"

"It'll be perfect for our project tonight," I said.

That night when the croppers looked at me expectantly, I explained that our make-and-take would combine a new skill and upcycling, which is a fancy word for turning something old into something new. "Because every scrapbooker needs help staying organized, I thought we'd turn these empty cans into pencil cups. If you're like me, you have handfuls of colored pencils. You have to dig through them to find the right color."

The women looked skeptical. Lottie Feister in particular. But I showed them my example. "See? I tangled a simple Zentangle pattern on a piece of brown kraft paper. I wrapped the strip of paper around the can, coated it with Mod Podge, and isn't it gorgeous?"

Of course it was, and my crafters were thrilled with my project. As I had explained to Dodie, the kraft paper was tougher than our scrapbook paper. It had more tensile strength. After the crafters drew their designs, they were able to glue the kraft paper to the empty cans. Because of its durability, they could easily wrap it around the ridges in the cans. By pinching down the cut edge of the can, where the lid had been joined to the body, we made sure there weren't any sharp surfaces. But to be extra careful, I had the scrapbookers wrap the excess kraft paper over the cut edges of the cans.

Not only did the finished products look cool, the kraft paper was durable enough to withstand the rough usage that the can would get as an organizing container.

Shortly after midnight, the last customers walked out our front door. "You, Kiki Lowenstein, are a force of nature," Dodie said. "I would have never come up with such a weird and wonderful idea."

"Not to mention cheap."

At that she laughed.

CHAPTER 21

Saturday morning...

While I was at the crop, Mert had left me a text message that we'd rendezvous the next morning at Marla Lever's house. Six a.m. is early, even for me. Fortunately, my daughter had opted for a sleep-over at her friend Nicci Moore's house, so I didn't have to disturb my kid when I woke up at early.

The city streets were deserted when I pulled up in front of the house in Ladue. Mert, and her brother Johnny were already there. One of her friends, Trudy Squires, joined us shortly.

Mert knows a lot of people, partially because she's been in the cleaning business so long. Trudy, I gathered, was a single woman between jobs and husbands. I'd put her age at mid-thirties. Unlike me, Trudy was skinny as a stick. The excessive amount of hair flipping signaled that Trudy was on the prowl as she cast flirtatious eyes toward Johnny. I couldn't blame her. Johnny had that whole "bad boy" vibe going for him. He'd spent time up in Petosi for a crime he didn't commit, and the stint behind bars produced a tough, man's man. But behind that macho exterior was a heart of gold, a sweet guy who'd been after me to go on dates with him.

I couldn't. My heart belonged to Detweiler, and now it ached every time I saw the cop. I figured it wasn't fair to Johnny to date him if we had no future. Treating Johnny as a distraction would be unkind—and he deserved more. With time, I could get over Detweiler. At least, that's what I hoped. To encourage me to forget him, Sheila had her sights on a man she considered a suitable suitor for me, Ben Novak. I'll give her this: my mother-in-law has an eye for good-looking men. Ben looks like he belongs on the cover of a Ralph Lauren catalogue. He's tall, blond, and buff.

Unfortunately, he isn't Detweiler.

"Put this on over your duds." Mert interrupted my thoughts as she handed me a white Tyvek biohazard suit with sleeves gathered at the wrists and the ankles. Over our shoes we slipped white Tyvek booties. Just when I thought it couldn't get any weirder, Mert passed us latex gloves and hoods with gas masks. We looked like a convention of astronauts.

"Gonna be hotter than blue blazes in there," said our fearless leader. Somehow she managed to get all her earrings inside her hood, but I can't imagine how. As for the heat, I was already feeling trickles of perspiration running under my arms.

"Listen up and listen good. I got window and room air conditioning units going inside, but when you're wearing these, you generate your own sauna. I cain't take the chance on any of you getting sick on me. So I'm setting out the rules and I expect you to obey them."

I'd never heard her act like General Patton before. I expected to see an American flag rise behind her as she lectured us.

"Three rules: Rule Number One—At twenty-minute intervals, this here alarm clock will sound. I expect you to stop your work, go outside, sit on a lawn chair, pull off your mask, and drink down a bottle of water. No exceptions."

"By the time you get thirsty, you're already dehydrated," Mert said. "I can't have you fainting on me. So all of you will come out here and drink water, while I watch you do it. The temperature is supposed to stay lower this morning and afternoon, but with all the work you'll do and these suits, you still risk dehydration.

"Rule Number Two—Never remove the filtering mask or the gloves while indoors. Never ever." Mert's hands moved in a gesture designed to underscore her last point. "I don't know what we're dealing with here. You've all had your hepatitis and tetanus shots, so you're good to go, but I do not want to put any of you at risk, so the mask and the gloves stay on. No matter what.

"Rule Number Three—Nothing leaves the premises. Valuables come to me. I'll log them and lock them up. We'll start with clearing out the trash and putting it in this Dumpster for the police to check once more before they release it. If you see something unusual, something that don't seem right, call me. There was a murder on this here piece of land, so keep your eyes open. The police have been through the place with a fine tooth comb, but that don't mean we won't find nothing. Iff'n you do, let me know. ASAP. Now get to it."

"I thought that because the police had released the scene, we didn't need to worry." I was surprised by how muffled my voice was.

"They're human, and they make mistakes like we all do. I jest don't want to get crosswise with Detective Grumpy Pants."

"You mean Hadcho?"

"Yeah, him. Let's get moving," said Mert.

The hoods blocked our peripheral vision, which caused all four of us to move clumsily, at least at first. My hands are tiny, and my gloves stuck out past my fingers, making grasping stuff hard. The suits weren't uncomfortable in themselves. Rather like wearing a FedEx mailing envelope, I guess. (Although I haven't done that, I've seen some photos of fashion projects where students did exactly that.) Mainly, their generous proportions proved awkward, especially for me. After I tripped twice on my own pants, Mert grabbed a roll of duct tape from her truck and adjusted my hems.

"That better?" she asked.

"Yes." The worst part of this weird get-up was the sense of claustrophobia it caused, coupled with the ongoing irritation of fumbling about.

Mert assigned me the job of gathering up newspapers, tying them with string, and carrying them to the recycling bin. Starting at the front door, I managed to clear the foyer before we took our first break. My back and arms ached pleasantly, the way muscles do when you are getting good exercise. But my lower back started in with sharp pangs. The pain was a prelude to spasms; I stopped and took a couple of Advil.

"You, okay?" Mert came over to my side when she noticed me at the watering station, gulping down the reddish pills.

"Yep." No way was I bailing out on her.

Getting the newspapers out of the living room would present a challenge. I'd have to carry the heavy bales of newspaper through the small foyer and out the front door. That would slow me down and put more strain on my muscles.

What to do, what to do?

Opening a window was the best idea. I could toss the newspaper bundles out of the window, run outside, and haul them to the recycling bin. But when I tried to yank on the sills, I snapped off two fingernails, down to the quick.

"Ouch!" I squealed in pain.

"What's the matter, little girl? That window too much for you?" With one hand, Johnny popped loose one of the closed windows. "Not much to do in prison other than work out."

"Thanks," I told him.

"Cost you a kiss," he said.

I laughed and pecked him on the cheek, which was really weird with our helmets bumping and our masks shielding our skin. We would never be more than friends, but I thought the world of the man. He seemed determined to walk a narrow path, to pay back his big sister for all his legal fees, and to make Mert proud of him. Consequently, whenever she needed help on a big job, he was Johnny-on-the-spot, and that was no joke.

"You're planning to toss them papers out the window, aren't you?" He sized up the situation. "That's a good idea. Let me open the other three windows so you'll get a breeze and so's you don't have to walk so far with the bundles. Mert told me you have asthma. She said I better keep an eye on you. The outside air'll be better than what's in here, but if you need me, just holler."

"You okay?" Mert noticed Johnny talking with me. "How's your asthma?"

I didn't want to tell her that I'd already used my inhaler twice, so I lied and said, "Fine, but the open windows will help a lot." The A/C in Marla's house was largely ineffective. The fan couldn't blow cool air through the stacks and piles of paper. Was it possible that she didn't even know the A/C had gone out? Maybe she's grown accustomed to the stale, stinking, hot air, but on that particular day, it had overcome her.

As I worked, the day moved from warm to beastly hot. Sweat dripped down my face. When I bent over to wrap string around the papers, the salty liquid rolled into my eyes. Instinctively, I tried to wipe it away, but of course, the Tyvek didn't absorb anything.

At some point, I yanked the curtains to one side to allow the maximum air flow. As I lifted my arms, my back screamed long and loudly with pain, the spasms taking their toll. I stood up, pressing against my lower lumbar and using my knuckles to relieve the muscles.

Something landed on the top of my head.

I whooped with fear, batting at my hood with both hands.

No one heard me because everyone else was busy in other corners of the house. Trudy in the back bedroom. Johnny in the garage. Mert in the kitchen.

That thing on my head slipped to one side. Tiny pinpricks stabbed through the Tyvek and into my scalp. A tiny yellow paw appeared as I looked through the lenses of my goggles. I held perfectly still.

What had landed on my head?

I stood perfectly still, but the thing on my Tyvek helmet moved. Could it be that I'd been bombarded by a stray cat? Had we overlooked one?

But this thing on my head was far too light to be a cat. It couldn't weigh more than a few ounces.

I strained my ears and was rewarded by the tiniest "meow" ever. Slowly I moved my hands upwards and plucked from my head a palm-sized yellow tabby. He stared at me with big lime-green eyes and tried to "meow" again but nothing came out.

"You poor little tyke. They rounded up everyone else, didn't they? Let's see what we can do for you."

I carried the kitten over to Mert, who'd been working in Marla's bedroom. We walked outside. She pulled off her hood and shook her head. I did the same. She glanced down at the kitten and gave me a glum look. "He'll probably die."

"W-w-what?" I cradled the cat to my chest. "What do you mean, die? He'll be okay. He has to."

"Most of Marla's cats were sick." Mert stared at the tiny ball of yellow fluff. "If this one don't have feline distemper, it's a miracle. You can't take him home because he'll only kick the kitty litter bag on you—and that would break your heart."

"He'll make it. You can tell he's a fighter. His name is Martin." I don't know why I called him "Martin," but it fit.

"Martin, huh? Change outta your biohazard suit and drive him over to the shelter. See what they say, then get right back here."

On the ride over, Martin curled up in my lap and purred happily. Handing the tiny cat over to Mrs. Gershin, the shelter volunteer, nearly did me in. Martin didn't want to let me go. He gripped me with his claws and mewed weakly, while Mrs. Gershin and I tried to disentangle him from my clothes.

The elderly volunteer wrinkled her nose behind big trifocal glasses that magnified her eyes to comic proportions. "Yours? You giving him up?"

"Gosh, no." I explained who I was and how I found him.

"Sad day. We've put twenty-two cats to sleep already." She held up Martin with one hand and examined him carefully. "Very young. I'd guess he's two weeks old. See how his ears are still folded over? This one will need to be hand-fed."

"I'll do it. I'll hand feed him."

"You want to get up every four hours?"

I swallowed hard. "No, but I will."

"Hey there, little boy," cooed Mrs. Gershin.

"His name is Martin."

Mrs. Gershin's tiny smile blossomed into a big grin. "You're sunk. Once you name them, you claim them."

I figured as much. "I have to get back to work."

"We close at five. Come back then. I'll give you instructions for feeding Martin. We'll have the vet check him. You do know you'll have to encourage his bowels to move, don't you?"

"I've probably encouraged bowel movements in the past. But not on purpose."

"Let's see if we can perfect your technique."

CHAPTER 22

On the way back to Marla's, I stopped at my house and let out the dogs. I talked to Petunia and Gracie about Martin, and explained, "Of course, I can't be sure that he's coming home with me. I mean, um…"

I didn't tell them he might not make it, because I didn't want to upset them. Instead, after checking on their water and letting them run around outside a bit, I hopped back in my car and bought a round of Wendy's Frosties for my co-workers. As we spooned up our confections, I told them about Martin.

"Want to hear the calorie count on the Frosties?" asked Trudy, tapping away at her iPhone. No wonder she was so skinny.

"No," we answered in chorus.

"Kiki Lowenstein, you are some kind of fool, adopting that kitten," Mert said. "You need another mouth to feed like you need a tattoo of a sailor on your right boob."

"I'd pay to see that." Johnny leered at me. "In fact, I'd pay for the tat."

"While Kiki found a kitty, guess what I found?" Trudy undid the scrunchy holding back her hair, shook it out, and put it back up in a high ponytail.

"Can't be as cool as what I uncovered. There's an old motorcycle squeezed behind Mrs. Lever's car. I mean, that thing is museum old! There's also about a zillion plus tools. Ever' thing you could ever want, like staplers, wood shavers, blades, jigs, and carving tools." Johnny beamed with manly appreciation at Marla's collection.

"Ain't nothing compared to the upstairs bedroom," said Trudy. "It looks like some sort of shrine to a little boy."

"Must have belonged to her son Anthony," I said.

"There's a made-up bed," continued Trudy, "and his shoes

piled on top of each other like he slipped them off, and he'll be back any minute. Cool comic books from the 70s. An old train system. Imagine a boy's room forty years ago, and you'll get the picture. They could use it in Hollywood for a sitcom set. I just love those old TV shows, don't you?"

Trudy set down her iPhone and poured a little of her water over her neck. I gestured toward the back of my head, and she dumped a splash on me.

"You-all need to take photos, hear me?" Mert handed around disposable cameras. "Trudy, I'll come document the kid's room first. Johnny? Take them flattened boxes and papers outta the garage, but don't move any tools until I see 'em and log 'em."

"Yes, Sis." Johnny gave her a mock salute.

He was interrupted by a gold Lexus SUV swinging into the driveway. A nicely dressed woman in her late fifties climbed out, taking care to step down from the high vehicle in a ladylike manner. Although she moved like a person accustomed to being in charge, her face showed signs of distress with dark circles and puffy skin under reddened eyes.

"That's our boss," Mert said. We all stood up and stepped forward, ready to meet Ali Timmons.

"Are you taking a break?" Mrs. Timmons scowled at us and checked her wristwatch. "It's only a little after eleven."

"Yes, ma'am," Mert said. "These suits cause dehydration. I make my people take mandatory breaks for water. You don't want someone fainting. Not in there. It's too dangerous. Those piles of papers could come down."

"Why must you wear those? You …you make this situation look worse than it is." Mrs. Timmons' hands were clenched into tight fists.

"Ma'am? It's a biohazard," Mert said. "Your mother's house is covered with animal feces. There's vermin there, too, drawn to the garbage she collected. Have you been inside?"

"No, not in a long while."

"I suggest you walk in and take a look around. That way you'll have a better idea of what we're dealing with."

We watched as Mrs. Timmons mounted the steps. She straightened her shoulders, threw us a defiant look, opened the door, and stepped inside. Since I'd cleared the foyer, she was able to walk past the vestibule and into the living room.

"One Mississippi, two Mississippi, three Mississippi, four Mississippi," Johnny counted.

When he got to "eleven Mississippi," Ali Timmons ran out of the house and screamed, "A rat! I saw a rat as big as a cat!"

"I'm on it." Johnny trotted to his truck, grabbed a jumbo version of a snap mousetrap, and headed toward the house.

Mrs. Timmons began to blubber as she moved to one side to let him pass. "I told her! I begged her! She wouldn't listen to me. How many times must we go through this? Ever since my brother died, she's been like this. Dad gave up and left us. I was only eight. Can you imagine what it was like growing up in a house like this?"

"Come on over here and have a seat." Mert took our employer by the arm. "Let us get you some nice cold water."

Mrs. Timmons kept talking, muttering words that made little sense. Mert soothed her, telling her it wasn't her fault, that we would get it all cleaned up, and promising not to let anything of value leave the premises.

"Mom used to have nice silver. I think it's all gone. We had Granddad's woodworking tools, and I don't know if they're still there or not. They were nice antiques. Everything of value is gone. She sold it to buy cat food. Cat food! I quit talking to her because I got so angry. She would buy things, weird things. I'd ask her, 'What will you do with that?' and she'd say, 'I have plans.' That was always it. She had plans!"

"I won't let nothing get tossed. We're photographing everything, and all the rubbish is going into the Dumpster. But we won't remove it from the premises until you say so. That way you can sort through it. I promise. Kiki is bundling up the newspapers and tossing them out the windows. That way we'll have a clear path. We can videotape and photograph every inch of the place so you look over what've you got."

Mert didn't add that we'd also be making a record that the police could use, but Mrs. Timmons caught the drift.

"My mother wouldn't hurt a flea. She couldn't have killed anyone. I think someone planted that body in the freezer. Mom's not strong enough to lift anyone."

"Yes, ma'am. I'm sure the cops will figure it out," Mert said.

I tossed my empty water bottle in the recycling bin and went over to Mrs. Timmons. "Ma'am? Your mother has been coming to the scrapbook store where I work. She's brought in photos of you and your brothers. We were working on putting them in an album as part of a class I'm teaching at the store. I'll make sure to get them back to you."

After Ali Lever Timmons thanked me, I walked into the house and started bundling newspapers again. We worked steadily all afternoon, taking breaks only for water and Advil. At the end of the day, we pulled off our Tyvek suits and hung them up in Marla's garage. Mert had decreed that Sunday would be a day of rest for all of us.

"I have to work Monday morning at the scrapbook store," I told Mert as we said goodbye.

"No problem. Come on over here when you get done."

"Will do."

CHAPTER 23

Saturday evening...

On my way home, I swung by the Animal Shelter. Mrs. Gershin winked at me as she handed over a tiny baby bottle and three cans of cat formula. "These are samples we had in the back. That ought to get him through the next week. He should be able to make the switch to regular food by then. Here's a sheet with instructions."

I thanked her and carried away my new friend in the cardboard cat carrier Mrs. Gershin had thoughtfully supplied. Boy, was Anya going to be surprised!

When we got to my house, I let the dogs sniff the outside of the cardboard carrier. Through holes in the top, I saw Martin respond by hissing and puffing up to twice his original size.

Mrs. Gershin had warned me, "Even if he doesn't hiss and spit, that doesn't mean Martin isn't scared. Being afraid of dogs is instinctive. You'll need to introduce him to the other animals slowly."

I wanted our new friend to feel secure in his new home. The best place for Martin and his carrier was in my bedroom. I had just closed the door on my bedroom when my doorbell rang.

Detweiler stood on my front step looking awkward. "Have you eaten?"

"Nope."

"I could order a pizza."

"Twist my arm," I said and grinned. It's against my religion to turn down food. "You order the pizza, and I'll make us a salad, how's that? I want to hear what you've learned about Marla Lever."

Thirty minutes later, Detweiler graciously offered to let me keep the slices we didn't eat. I cleared the dishes, while he sat at my kitchen table nursing a cold glass of iced tea.

"I'd like to share a few details with you, if you don't mind," he said in a terribly formal way. "They'll appear in the newspaper tomorrow, so it's not like I'm leaking state secrets. But since you know Mrs. Lever, and since she's still in a coma, I thought you might also know the victim, the dead woman whose body was found in the freezer."

"Okay." I wrapped the leftover pieces in foil.

"If you do, you might also know something about the nature of their relationship."

That sounded weird, but I kept my mouth shut and filled the dishwasher.

"The dead woman has been identified as one Sandra Newcomber. She and Marla Lever got into it a few months back. Here, let me help with that." Detweiler dried the salad bowl while I washed our plates. "By the way, where's your daughter?"

"She's spending the night at her best friend Nicci Moore's house. I usually don't let her sleep over two nights in a row, but the girls were working on an art project together."

He sank down into a chair, realizing as I did, that we were alone together — if you didn't count the watchful eyes of Gracie, and Petunia.

Awkward. My heart pounded faster. Every nerve in my body was charged with electricity. The unspoken words between us created friction. I needed to move around, to keep at bay the restless feelings inside me. I grabbed a box of brownie mix and gathered ingredients.

He's off-limits, I told myself. Obviously he's having problems with his marriage, but he belongs to his wife. I should do everything I can to avoid him.

But that was impossible! Especially since my husband's killer was on the lam. From time to time, I still got ugly messages in my mailbox. There were hang-up calls on my phone. Once I came home to a bloody mess on my porch, a clear warning that the killer hadn't forgotten about me.

To be honest, I wasn't sure whether Detweiler and I could just be friends. It seemed too difficult for both of us. For a while, I had been successful at avoiding the man, but the ill-advised crop at Marla Lever's house had given us a new reason to reconnect. Now we were two adults thrown together by an impossible situation. We had reason to talk to each other, right?

Right. And if you eat food in the dark, the calories don't count.

"Why did Marla Lever get into it with Mrs. Newcomber in the first place?"

"Not surprisingly, there was a hassle over a cat. Mrs. Newcomber's pet had slipped past her and raced out of the front door before she could grab it. She called and called, but the cat didn't come back. However, that's where the story takes a wrong turn. Mrs. Lever claimed the cat showed up at her front door one day. According to Marla Lever, she was a good Samaritan who took in a starving, homeless stray. Problem being, she never made any attempt to find the owner, her neighbor, Mrs. Newcomber."

"If there wasn't any identification, maybe Marla really thought the cat had been dumped." I cracked an egg against the side of the mixing bowl.

"That's another problem with her story. Other neighbors remembered Mrs. Newcomber going from house to house asking after her cat. In fact, according to at least one neighbor, Mrs. Newcomber was incredibly persistent about knocking on doors and checking for her lost pet. Mrs. Newcomber stapled color posters with pictures of her cat to nearby telephone poles. At the very least, you could say that Mrs. Lever didn't bother to look hard for cat's owner."

"But Marla turned the cat over when she found out it belonged to Mrs. Newcomber, right?"

"No, she did not. Mrs. Newcomber knew Marla Lever had a

house full of cats. That was common knowledge in their neighborhood. She kept stopping by Mrs. Lever's house, asking if she'd seen the lost pet. On her third visit, when Mrs. Lever opened her door, Mrs. Newcomber's cat came flying out, trying to get to her owner. But Mrs. Lever was faster than Mrs. Newcomber. Marla Lever snatched up the cat and refused to give the animal back to Mrs. Newcomber. She claimed the animal had been abandoned and that she'd rescued it."

I mixed the batter, putting a lot of muscle into the process. This story was getting worse and worse by the minute. Sure, I'd known all along that Marla Lever was odd. But I never figured her for a liar and a thief. Was it possible that she was also a murderer?

"Did I mention that Mrs. Newcomber's cat was wearing a collar with a tag attached when it first ran off? That tag was engraved with Mrs. Newcomber's cell phone number."

I stopped my stirring. "You have to be kidding."

"No, I'm not. The cat was still wearing the collar when an Animal Control Officer went to the house and retrieved the animal."

"I bet the fur started flying over that." I glanced at my kitchen clock. "Time for Martin's ten o'clock feeding."

"Martin?"

"A kitten. He landed on my head while I was cleaning, and I decided to keep him. He has to eat every four hours."

"Do you seriously expect to get up again at two?" Detweiler asked. "And then again at six? How will you function at work? Especially after spending all day working in that house in this heat?"

"I have no idea." I excused myself and walked past him to my bedroom where I retrieved the cardboard cat carrier. Gracie paid no attention to the kitten when I came back, because Detweiler was rubbing her ears.

Petunia had fallen asleep under the table and didn't even look up as I set the carrier on my empty seat.

"Actually, I'm not as worried about how I'll manage at work as I am about getting Martin to poop. I'm supposed to dampen a cotton balls and rub his kitty bits until he feels the urge."

"Kitty bits? Cotton balls?" Detweiler doubled over laughing.

"Ha, ha, ha. When you are old and having trouble pooping don't come crying to me, buddy. You'll be alone and on your own." I didn't look at him. I couldn't.

"Kiki? We need to talk about Brenda, my wife."

I shook my head violently. "No, we do not. That topic is off the table. Seriously. You're a married man and that's that. You're here tonight because I might have information that can solve a murder case. That's it; that's all. When this is over, we go our separate ways."

"If that's what you want."

My voice broke as I said, "That's what I want, what I expect, and how it has to be."

CHAPTER 24

"I guess I better get going. I have files I need to review for a cold case we're investigating." Detweiler stood to leave, but he hesitated, glancing over at Martin who was squirming in my hands. "Have you done this before?"

"Fed and taken care of a baby cat like this? Nope. Mert doesn't expect Martin to live, so I hope I'm doing everything the right way."

"My mom used to do this with animals on the farm. When we got old enough, we'd take a turn, too. How about if I heat the formula for you?"

"That would be a big help," I admitted. Even though Gracie was disinterested and Petunia was oblivious, Martin smelled the dogs, and he was scared. Mewling loudly, he sank his tiny needle-sharp claws into my arms as he tried to climb up, up, up and away.

Detweiler turned on the tap. Checking the water temp, he held the tiny plastic bottle beneath the running water. As I waited, he rotated the bottle left, then right, and left again.

"Care to talk about your cold cases?" I asked. "I'm a good listener. Besides, it'll take Martin a while to drink his formula."

"I don't want to share too much with you," he said. "It's the stuff of nightmares."

"You won't tell me anything? Even if I bribed you with a brownie for the road?"

"A brownie for the road sounds like a fair trade. All I can tell you is what's been reported in the news." After testing the temperature of the milk on the inside of his wrist, he handed the bottle to me. Then he sank back down into the chair he'd recently vacated. "For ten years now women have been disappearing all around St. Louis County. There doesn't seem to be a pattern. Often they'd gone out to eat or to a movie or to the mall or shopping. Their cars were found empty. Their purses were there, untouched. There's no sign of a struggle."

"That means they went with someone willingly."

"Or they were overpowered quickly, so that they couldn't fight."

"If they were overpowered, isn't it more likely that would have happened outside of their cars?"

"Yes."

"Then their purses would have probably been missing, too, since most of us wear purses over our shoulders."

"Right." He watched as I sat on the floor and put Martin in the diamond formed by my legs. Before I could feed the kitten, I needed to warm him up, which I did by lightly massaging him. I also put a few drops of formula on my fingers and rubbed this onto his lips to stimulate his appetite.

"Anything else? Any other similarities?"

"The women were all between the ages of thirty and fifty. All had dark hair. None of their bodies have turned up."

"What color hair did Sandra Newcomber have?" Detweiler watched as Martin settled down to do serious work on his bottle. The kitten looked adorable with a dab of milk on his chin. His tiny paws kneaded my leg rhythmically as he drank his dinner.

"Dark."

"Are you thinking another woman lured them into a car?"

"I don't know how the women were overpowered, but I will say this: You need to be careful, Kiki. Never park next to a van with a sliding door. Always stay aware of your surroundings. Have your keys ready when you go to your car. Get in, lock the door immediately, and then fuss with your seatbelt. Too many people get in, forget to lock the doors, and take their time adjusting their seatbelts and mirrors in an unlocked car."

"You really think Marla Lever was involved in this?" I looked up into those amazing green eyes of his and saw doubt.

"You don't, do you?"

Martin was done with his bottle. I held him against my shoulder like I used to hold Anya. With tiny pats to his back, I encouraged him to burp.

Detweiler shook his head. "I don't, but I could be wrong. She's still unconscious. When she comes to, if she comes to, she'll have to go through rehab to regain her ability to talk or write. Who knows how long it might take for her to respond to our questions? If she ever does."

"But she couldn't have done all that herself." Now I needed to play Mama Cat and give Martin a quick bath. Using a fresh washcloth, I wet it with warm water, wrung it out, and wiped the kitten down. Next I dried him with a gentle massage, using a fresh dry washcloth. After stimulating his kitty bits, and getting the desired result, I cleaned him again before carefully drying him off.

"You're putting a lot of time and attention in one little guy who may or may not make it," Detweiler said.

"Isn't that what life is all about? Taking chances? Giving time and love and attention to people, things, and situations that might not pan out? That's the definition of hope, and without hope, life would be too bleak for me."

It was more revealing than I would have liked, but once the words were out there, I couldn't take them back.

I wrapped a chunk of brownies for Detweiler. "Getting back to Marla Lever, I can't figure out how she would have shoved a body into her freezer. You didn't say how big Sandra Newcomber was, but Marla couldn't weigh more than 140. Her arms were flabby. It wasn't like she worked out and could bench press her body weight."

"She wouldn't be the first killer to pair up with a man. Or even another woman. History is full of killing duos. Usually the dominant personality persuades the weaker one to join in."

"That might have happened, but I don't see it. Marla acted

like a loner. To me, she seemed like a harmless cat lover who'd gone cuckoo for coconuts. But I guess that's why serial killers are so lethal. They blend in, right?"

Detweiler's smile was tight. "I hope she's just a harmless older woman with a hoarding problem. That would be bad enough. Because if she is part of a murderous twosome..."

I finished his sentence for him: "The other half is still out there."

CHAPTER 25

Detweiler's departure was abrupt. He stood up quickly, like a jack-in-a-box pops up when the lid is released. "I'll be going," he said, and he beat me to the front door.

After his taillights faded in the night, I realized we'd both come to the same conclusion: We couldn't be trusted alone with each other. That scared me. A lot. I crawled into bed and stared at my ceiling for a long, long time.

The next morning before Jennifer Moore dropped off my daughter, I invited her child, Nicci, to stay overnight and spend Sunday with us. Jennifer happily agreed to the plan, and two hours later, she pulled up in her blue Mazda Miata to let the girls out.

The pre-teen girls squealed with excitement when I told them about Martin.

"A kitten! Oh, Mom! Is this one from that animal hoarder?" Anya shrieked with joy.

"Yes. This little guy actually landed on my head. He's just a baby, so we have to go slowly introducing him to Gracie and Petunia. That's why he's still in his carrier box and back in my bedroom. I'll show you how we need to take care of him. Also, I have to warn you that he might not make it. He's had a tough start in life."

"He'll make it." Anya leveled determined eyes at me. "I'm sending him love and good vibes."

I hoped that would be exactly what Martin needed.

The girls were fascinated, watching Martin suck on his tiny bottle. Anya asked to hold him, but Nicci wasn't interested. My kid is nutty for critters, while Nicci is a budding fashionista who's more interested in mall shopping. Even so, the girls are good friends.

"The bottle's empty; it's time to burp him like a baby. After that, I need to get his insides moving." In preparation, I dampened a cotton ball.

"Totally gross." Nicci made a face.

She was right, but her lack of enthusiasm didn't make a difference to my daughter.

"He's so cute!" While Anya watched me stroking the kitten, she told me all about summer camp. "We're doing these cool black and white drawings. It's to learn about optical illusions. I told our teacher about your Zentangle art, Mom. Could you come to class and teach us how?"

"Of course. Zentangle makes a larger than normal tile called The Apprentice that's perfect for kids."

Nicci smiled indulgently at Anya. Crafty stuff wasn't her bag. I wondered how long they would remain friends. In many ways, large and small, they were very different. However, in one big way, they were the same—they both loved their mothers. Nicci's dad was a jerk, to put it mildly. But Nicci and Jennifer were close. Very close. Maybe that would be enough of a common trait to nurture the girls' friendship.

I had been keeping one eye on the kitchen clock. "Time for soccer practice."

The kids changed into their practice duds quickly, while I grabbed cold bottles of water from my refrigerator. I'd taken to saving glass bottles with plastic lids. Unlike plastic bottles, these could be sterilized between uses, filled with water, and then the process could be repeated. I felt good about recycling and saving money.

We loaded the dogs into the car. It was a bit cramped, so Petunia sat on Anya's lap and Gracie perched regally in the front passenger's seat. When I pulled up to stop lights, other drivers did a double-take at the massive black and white head next to mine.

Detweiler showed up at the practice field with two tall plastic cups of iced green tea from Bread Co. and a couple of pumpkin muffies for us to share. Muffies are the tops of muffins. Originally they were sliced off, but now you can buy pans with shallow indentations and bake muffies yourself. If you like the crispy outside of a muffin more than the moist cake inside, you'll find muffies to be the perfect solution.

"Your brownies were great. I figured I owed you," he said, with a grin. "Since I'd noticed the practice schedule you had posted on your refrigerator with certain games highlighted in pink, I was pretty sure you'd be here."

"How can I complain about your prying eyes when you bring me food and drink?"

"I'm being used?"

"You know you are. Welcome to the world of being objectified. How was your day?"

"This cold case work is slow going," he said as he reached into a back pocket of his jeans and pulled out a folded sheet of paper. "I've listed all the traits the women have in common. Dark hair, same general body type, roughly the same age. Otherwise I can't find any common denominators. I re-interviewed one victim's best friend. You can read the report. Maybe you'll see something I missed. It might be that I need a woman's take on this mess."

Julianna Rossini, a forty-four-year-old teacher, could have been any one of my scrapbookers. Newly single. Divorced. Mom of two. Loved line-dancing and country western music. Had two cats. Liked mysteries and romances. Went to the movies every Saturday with a friend.

A totally unremarkable life, in that sense of the word that implied nothing to call attention to her existence.

Detweiler added another sheet of folded paper to the one in my hands. "Here's the interview Hadcho did with another victim's sister."

Leesa Gainer had been a thirty-nine-year-old secretary.

Married. Three kids, a dog and a cat. Worked downtown. Liked to knit. Taught Sunday School. Then one day she was gone, baby, gone.

"You haven't found any sign of them? No bodies?"

"Nada. It's like — *poof* — they disappeared into thin air."

I swallowed a lump in my throat. We'll all leave this earth one day, but how sad it would be to miss out on the chance to tell your loved ones goodbye. Worse yet, how horrible to be the one left behind, wondering if that other person was somewhere, hurt or suffering, and you couldn't help them. The unknowing would be incredibly painful.

"What's your working theory?"

"I'm stumped." As he rubbed the back of his neck, the clean scent of soap wafted my way. He always smelled like Safeguard soap with a hint of masculine cologne. Unlike a lot of men, he didn't drench himself in scent. "I keep thinking that as we go over the interviews, something will pop out at us. That we'll see some common thread that we can track down. Today I'm going to lock myself in the evidence room and comb through all the pieces we've collected. People think this is an exciting job, but most of it is tedium. I once solved a murder by realizing four numbers on a paper napkin were part of a phone number. That led us to a guy, and the thread unraveled from there. I owe it to these women's families to keep banging my head against the wall until I see the light."

I wouldn't have guessed about the tedium, but once he explained, it made sense. Going through the ephemera—tickets, receipts, canceled checks, lists, fliers, stubs, and so on—brought in by my scrapbookers certainly told me a lot about them and their lives. I could see how revisiting the evidence collected regarding each missing woman might do the same for Detweiler. By viewing my clients' paper trails, I learned where they shopped, how often they ate out and what they ordered, the kind of money they spent, and their habits in general.

"Would you like to look at the stuff Marla gave me?" I asked. "There might be something in there of interest. I planned to bundle everything up and return it to her daughter, but she didn't seem to be in any hurry to get it back."

"What sort of materials are you talking about?"

"Photos, calendars, checkbook stubs, bills." I explained how most of my students couldn't put their hands on such ephemera. "However, Marla was a champ. Man, oh, man, did she have tons of paperwork to draw on. Er, I don't mean drawing as in scribbling, I mean, as in using as a resource."

"That might be helpful."

For the next hour, he and I sat on the bench and cheered for the girls. During one break, Detweiler raced to Anya's side where he whispered in her ear. As a result, she scored two goals. Clearly, he'd offered her a little coaching that she'd taken to heart. Not for the first time did I regret that my daughter might grow up without a father. Especially one like Chad Detweiler. He whooped and hollered from the sidelines with the same intensity as the other dads in attendance, even though this was just a practice session and as such was sparsely attended. Most of the parents dropped their kids off and left. But a few stuck around. I liked practices because they were low key, and I used the time to get a little fresh air. Gracie sat diligently at my side, casting loving eyes at Detweiler, while Petunia snoozed under the bleachers.

When the coach dismissed the girls for the day, they raced over to us. Detweiler said, "I think a great practice like that deserves celebrating. How about some ice cream? Sheridan's has outdoor seating. We can bring the dogs."

He didn't have to ask twice. The girls jumped up and down with joy.

"Sorry," he said to me. "I should have asked your permission first."

"I'll forgive you this time," and I laughed.

By the time we finished our ice cream, said goodbye to Detweiler, and returned to my house, the girls were nodding off, even though they hadn't had any dinner. The exercise and the heat had tired them both out. They were hot, sweaty, and dust-covered.

"Go take your showers while I make us dinner." They came out scrubbed, sweet-smelling, and adorably wet behind the ears. I served them chicken and broccoli stir fry. All the food disappeared in record time, except for a cup and a half of rice that I'd turn into fried rice for another meal. After they ate, the girls settled onto the sofa where they fell fast asleep. I didn't rouse them. Instead, I tucked a blanket around the two of them and went to bed myself. I'd nearly nodded off when Mert rang my cell phone.

"I was on the horn with Ali for an hour." Mert sounded weary. "Her mom still is unconscious, so she's footing the bill for this clean up. I promised her if we found anything worth anything, we'd set it aside. She's hoping to have an estate sale, thinking that might help offset what I'll charge her."

"I'll be there as soon as I can on Monday."

"See you," she paused, "and thanks."

CHAPTER 26

Monday morning...

After dropping Nicci off at her home and Anya at the Science Center, the dogs, Martin, and I drove to Time in a Bottle. Not surprisingly, I was the first person there. I let the pooches roam the store while I got the place ready for the day. My chores included straightening and restocking shelves, checking for messages, and dusting everything. When I finished that, I put the dogs in the playpen and mopped the sales floor.

I had dumped a bucket of dirty water and put the mop away when I heard the back door slam. The off-key singing that followed announced Rebekkah had made it into work. She was, of course, an hour late, but that really wasn't my problem.

While she puttered around in her mother's office, I got busy taking care of Martin. We had our routine down pat. He latched onto the rubber nipple eagerly. With very little fuss and muss, I was the proud owner of an empty baby bottle, and his sweet little tummy bulged like a small pink balloon. Next came the process of swabbing Martin's nether parts with a damp cotton ball. He took it all in stride, but for one reason or another, I couldn't achieve the desired end result. I dampened a second cotton ball and tried again. I was concentrating on stroking his kitty bits when I heard Rebekkah's heavy footfall, so like her mother's. However, I didn't look up until she stood right in front of me. Us. Martin and me.

Before my eyes, Rebekkah's face changed from sullen to happy.

"A kitten! Get out! He's totally adorable. Where did you get him?"

I explained how he'd landed on my head. Rebekkah watched as Martin finally gave in to my stroking and did his business. Instead of being grossed out, she volunteered to take a turn feeding and stimulating him.

As a gesture of goodwill, I yielded Martin to her embrace. She cuddled the tiny fellow gently. I decided to take advantage of her good mood by taking the first step toward an improved relationship.

"We need to talk. You and I have always gotten along. I'd like to go back to that. I know you aren't happy. Is there anything I can do to make things better for you? I miss being your friend."

I held my breath and waited. Either she would recognize and respond to my sincerity or she'd get huffy, and we'd have a miserable day. For the longest time, she didn't answer. When I'd almost concluded she wasn't speaking to me, she glanced up from Martin, who was cuddled against her chest and purring.

"I'm such a screw-up." Her eyes, hazel like her mother's, filled with tears. "I should have never left Missou. But I didn't know what to do, and I didn't want to waste more of my parents' money. I was worried about my mom."

Touching her arm, I said, "I don't blame you. We're all concerned about her health."

"I hate working here in the store. I hate it! I'm not good at crafts. I never have been, and it makes me angry how stupid I look when I can't do stuff as good as you do."

"It's not true that you aren't good at crafts. You just don't put much effort into them. But that's not the real problem, is it?"

The tears started to fall. I brought her a box of tissues, ran to the refrigerator and returned with a Diet Coke for her.

"We're two savvy people," I said as I popped the tab on her cola. "We can't do anything to help your mom, but we can brainstorm ideas for you, right? I mean, if you could do anything—anything at all—and you knew you couldn't fail, what would that be?"

"I dunno." She sniffled.

"You can do better than that."

"I like helping people. Not with crafts, although that's all right, I guess. But I like talking to people. Hearing about their problems. Back at school, everyone called me 'The Counselor' because I was good at helping people sort things out." Her laugh was rueful. "That's such a crock because I can't help myself."

"Tell me the last time you lost track of everything because what you were doing was so intriguing."

"My sorority volunteered to help out at Big Sisters. I worked with a little girl to help her with her reading. That was totally awesome."

From there we talked about more ways Rebekkah could get involved in charity work. That led us to her considering the field of social work. Next I helped her create a list of agencies whose directors I'd met through scrapbooking. "Why don't you go on an informational interview with them? Use my name."

"What's an informational interview?" she asked.

It's easy to forget how young someone is. Or what we know. We all take our body of knowledge for granted as if those facts and skills came with our genetic code. Of course, they didn't. We acquired the information one piece at a time from this source and that, from this experience, and that overheard conversation, from watching other people struggle and succeed, and sometimes from watching others fail.

I explained that she could ask her interviewees what they studied in college, what skills they use in their jobs, what skills they wish they had, what a typical day was like, and what challenges they could foresee coming down the pike for their industries or associations.

"That makes sense. I could also ask them what they look for in a new hire." Rebekkah stroked Martin's back while she thought this over.

"Yes, and remember, there always changes on the horizon. A college education is a degree in learning, not an end-all and be-all. But I can tell you as someone who dropped out of school, I regret not having that degree every day of my life."

"Why? You do pretty well for yourself. You aren't making the money a doctor or lawyer might, but I guess there are plenty of unemployed English majors. At least that's what Garrison Keillor says."

"With a degree, you'll earn $1.3 million more in your lifetime. Four years isn't that big of an investment of time, and certainly the cost pays for itself. Besides that, a college degree gives a person confidence. When I was a kid, a high school diploma was the standard. Now it's that four-year degree. While in some ways I know it's silly, I look around when I'm at a gathering, and I think I'm probably the only person there who is uneducated. It puts a real crimp in my self-esteem. Let's not debate whether it should or not. Just trust me on this."

While Rebekkah called around to schedule her interviews, I made good on my promise to Detweiler by rounding up all of Marla Lever's photos and scrapbook materials. Fortunately, that didn't take long. Because we work with so many scrapbookers and their photos, we had developed a good system for keeping materials straight.

Actually, one of our customers was the first to show me how she used new, clean, and empty pizza boxes for storing photos and papers. The boxes were labeled with the names of each scrapbooker so they could easily be seen when the containers were stacked in alphabetical order. Each box served as a miniature storage locker, holding photos, journals, paper supplies, and ephemera the scrapper planned to put in an album. This proved especially helpful for the "My Life Highlights" class I'd been teaching.

Marla's photos were pretty much as I remembered them. I studied the subjects and their spatial positions, a clue to people's relationships. Marla's husband always stood to the far outside edge of any photo, his body not touching hers or anyone else's.

Marla always appeared with her arms draped over her children's shoulders. Ali and her brother Allen stood side-by-side, their faces nearly identical, with only their hairstyles making them distinctive. I hadn't realized the brother and sister were twins, and they took after their mother.

The other little Lever was the image of his dad, from his pointed nose to his round face and protruding ears. Anthony Lever stood on one foot, off-balance, posed mid-motion, his outline a bit blurred as if he hadn't been completely still when the picture was snapped.

This was one of the rare photos that Marla had narrated for me. "I always called him Anthony, not Tony. I hate how people slap nicknames on kids. My daughter is Allison, not Ali, and my son is Allen, not Al."

Inside the box was yet another artifact, a journal. Each scrapbooker had been encouraged to keep a diary for at least a month.

From this, my students would cull one twenty-four-hour period and build a page called "A Day in My Life." I pointed out that our lives change gradually, and we don't notice our new habits as they take the place of old ones. But when you compare a day today to a day ten years ago, you can see how your life has evolved.

Marla hadn't finished her "A Day in My Life" page. Her pizza box labeled "Marla Lever #1" held the paper I'd selected for our class project, along with the embellishments we were working on, and of course, her photos. I flipped through Marla's journal. Scribbling filled the pages. Much of the writing was too misshapen for me to decipher.

Using one of the exercises I offered, Marla had written diligently about her routine, from getting up in the morning through her completed daily activities.

A Day in the Life of Marla Lever

6:30 a.m.—Wake up.

7 a.m. – Defrosted ground meat in microwave. Mixed it with kibble. Put out in bowls.

7:30 a.m. – Made my coffee. Grocery list: More cat litter. Kibble. Creamora.

8 a.m. – Drove to Dierbergs. (Note: Car has funny rattle. Oil light is on--again.)

9 a.m.– Back to house.

9:30 a.m.– Visited (unintelligible).

Noon – Home for lunch.

1 p.m. – Checking out new resale shop and other sites.

5 p.m. – Dinner at Wendy's.

7:15 p.m. – A. came over. Brought back Blackie and more cat food. He'll do my lawn but his mower is broken. Thinks mine will work.

~*~

Each day from then on looked the same.

I assumed that A. was her son Allen. Otherwise she had no visitors; she lived a solitary life.

Most people don't keep a journal with any regularity. They find it too time-consuming. I do. There are ways to look back over your life, techniques I recommend in my classes. One is, "Locate your personal calendar or even your checkbook register for the past year. Those entries will tell you what you did, who you saw, and so on. If you have dates with no activity, go back and look at your credit card statement. Your statement not only records the dollar amount of your purchase, it can remind you what you bought. Of course, your buying habits will change as time goes on, but those purchases are clues as to what was happening in your life."

Some of my students had trouble coming up with any documents at all, but not Marla. She brought in her calendar from the past year, as well as calendars for many years back, her check register, and her credit card statements. She even had all her canceled checks and receipts. In fact, she astonished me and the rest of the class by bringing in a stack of papers clearly used as her "to do" lists. She had so much paper, I'd assigned a second pizza box to Marla just so she could keep it organized, which is why the box I now examined had been labeled "Marla Lever #1." Right below it sat "Marla Lever #2."

Now I knew why she had been able to bring in all that junk. Marla'd never seen a piece of paper that she didn't want to keep!

Rummaging through the paperwork in Marla Lever #2, I noted a few of the receipts were for vet visits, going back several decades. Seems she'd owned at least one or two cats (maybe even three or four) for most of her life. Several notations on her calendars bore the message, "Call Devon – cat food!"

Was her son-in-law supplying her with cat food? Did that qualify as aiding and abetting a hoarder? Or was he performing a humanitarian mission? Did his wife know and accept the fact he was trying to help? Or was that a sore spot in their marriage?

The alarm chimed on my cell phone. I asked Rebekkah if she'd like a full explanation of how to play Mama Cat to Martin.

"Do you do the same thing over and over?"

"Every four hours. I'll bring him up front so we'll both be available if a customer drops in." I stopped and thought a second. "Hey? Could you do me a favor? I'm working with Mert this afternoon over at Marla Lever's house. Would you take care of Martin for me while I'm gone?"

"Love to. Anytime you bring Martin in, I'm glad to help. You want me to drop him by your house after work? Then Gracie and Petunia could stay here, and I could take the dogs to your place later."

"Could you? That would be really helpful."

"I don't mind."

"That would be super. When you get to my place, please be sure to put Martin inside his cardboard cat carrier and then set it on my bed and close the door behind you. He needs to feel safe. I don't want him to be frightened by Gracie and Tunie. I don't think they would hurt him, but it's better to be careful. Besides, we don't want Martin to start being afraid of dogs. He's had a hard enough life so far."

"No problem. Good thinking about keeping him in your bedroom with the door closed. I've heard you need to introduce a new pet slowly. They get upset about losing their status just like people do."

Hmmm. People losing their status. Was that what was happening between Bama and me? Probably. She and I had been at odds from the minute she first arrived. Maybe I needed to have a candid talk with her, too.

I shuddered.

The very thought of approaching Bama overwhelmed me. Baby steps. The best I could manage was baby steps. I'd made a good start with Rebekkah. My hours at the store would be much more pleasant if she and I got along better.

"Hey, kiddo, how would you like to have dinner with us? With Anya and me? Sheila is dropping her off at six thirty. Do you want to stick around after you bring the animals to my house? Wait for Anya to get home, me to shower, and then eat with us?"

"You sure? You're bound to be tired from working in this heat," Rebekkah said.

"You're right about that. It's exhausting, and I will be stinky, dirty, tired, and starving. So I'll definitely need to eat, and Anya will be thrilled to spend time with you."

"I'd love that."

Rebekkah had gone from sullen to sunny. Life was good.

CHAPTER 28

Because Rebekkah was in such a good mood, she let me leave the store early and head over to Marla Lever's house, where my co-workers had made remarkable progress. The overpowering stink had dissipated slightly, mainly because a lot of the animal waste had been dumped into big black garbage bags and taken to the Dumpster. Mert and Johnny had scooped up the many clumps scattered throughout the dwelling. "What a job that was. We used a snow shovel. Marla couldn't keep up with all the poop her cats produced. Nobody could."

Was I ever glad that I'd missed out on that portion of the job!

Stacks of newspapers awaited me in the living room. I tied them into bundles so I could toss them out the open window. When a dozen or so bundles piled up outside, I ran out of the house and carried my haul to the recycling bin. Half of the living room floor had been cleared using this technique. An hour into the work, and I was already exhausted. I told myself that besides putting money in my pocket, this job was burning mucho calories. I could eat whatever I wanted for dinner tonight. Too bad I couldn't afford much besides a frozen pizza in my fridge.

As I tied and toted, my mouth watered as I fantasized about a fresh pan of lasagna. When we stopped for lunch, I mentioned my pasta cravings to my co-workers while I chewed on my peanut butter and jelly sandwich.

"Too bad you didn't grab one of them packages of ground meat yesterday," said Mert, wolfing down a bologna and cheese. "They all went to waste. I wouldn't trust them today."

"A frozen Stouffer's dinner will do me just as well. I don't really have a good lasagna recipe."

"I could find one for you," Trudy said as she pulled out her iPhone and started playing with it. She'd daintily spooned out a diet yogurt as her meal. "A vegetarian one would be best. Fewer calories."

"Thanks...I think."

Trudy acted more like a teenager than a grown woman. She pulled the scrunchy out of her dark chestnut hair and shook it loose onto her shoulders, sending out a cloud of strawberry-scented perfume.

While Mert did a slow survey of our progress, Johnny ate a thick meatloaf sandwich and Trudy entertained us with her new phone. Apple should have hired her as a spokesperson. That girl was crazy about her new toy.

We hadn't rested in the shade for long when Mert said to Johnny, "Time for us to videotape our progress. You two ladies chug yourselves more water and rest up. We're heading into the heat of the day."

Since we'd taken down all the window treatments, Trudy and I could watch the brother and sister walk from room to room, opening all the doors and drawers. Johnny videotaped the house, taking particular care to go through each room slowly, while Mert directed his movements and scribbled in a notepad, diligently referencing any item that might have value. There wasn't much worth noting: a VCR, an old camera, a nice pair of binoculars, and a boom box.

But Mert was upbeat when she rejoined us. "You never know what folks'll think is important. Crazy stuff. I don't wanna take no chances. Anything that halfway looks good, I'm locking up in the truck."

Trudy and I had enjoyed a thirty-minute rest while Mert and Johnny were taking their tour of the house. The break in the physical activity had done me a world of good. I felt like I could manage another couple of hours.

"Here's your assignments," Mert said. "Kiki, go to the kitchen and see what you can do. Let's have you clean out the refrigerator and cabinets. If we don't get rid of any stored food soon, we'll be back to square one with the bad smells. Trudy?

You go upstairs. Start cleaning out the bedrooms. Johnny? I want you to tackle the garage."

I did as Mert asked. Marla's kitchen trash can was only half-full. Her refrigerator held a dozen eggs, a package of lunch meat, a container of moldy cottage cheese, a half a package of Velveeta, and a stale loaf of bread. Her refrigerator freezer was packed with more plastic baggies of ground beef, but I had no desire to take any of it home with me. Instead, I dumped all of it into a black Hefty garbage bag. On my way to the Dumpster, I told Mert what I'd found.

"More bags of ground beef. That's about it."

"Thanks for letting me know." Her gloves were off because she'd been fooling with the camera. She ran a shaking hand over her face. "I got to tell you, when we found that person in the freezer, it done freaked me out. I ain't thinking straight. I shoulda cleaned the refrigerator out right then and there. That meat'll smell something fierce if I don't get that bag you're holding out of here quick-like. I think I'll take it home with me tonight. My garbage pickup is Friday. The rest of this mess can stay in the Dumpster, but this here'll attract bugs."

"More bugs," I corrected her gently.

"More and more and more bugs."

In the pantry, I discovered cans of Campbell's soup in two varieties: beef with vegetable and chicken vegetable. Behind the tins was a half-empty box of generic rice. How many times had I resorted to pouring hot condensed soup over cooked rice to make a meal? Too many to count. As I put the cans and the rice into a bag, I realized that Marla and I had that in common. We both knew how to stretch our food budget. After I retrieved a jar of instant tea from the back of a top shelf, the cupboard was bare.

I opened all the other kitchen cabinets. Nothing there but Corelle dishes and glasses and cups in a pattern that suggested the set was decades old.

Ten pet food bowls of different shapes and colors sat in the drying rack in the sink. They'd been neatly washed. An automatic pet watering system sat in the corner of the kitchen. There was still water inside. The tank bubbled noisily as I carried it to the sink.

Five placemats decorated with "Meow!" and "This house guarded by an attack cat!" sat in a neat row in a drawer.

Given the scant number of mats, obviously the cats were supposed to eat in shifts. I wasn't sure how that worked, because I was fairly certain that cats would not appreciate the importance of standing in line and waiting their turns, but I could have been mistaken. Maybe Marla had them trained.

I stepped back and lingered in the doorway to stare at the empty kitchen. What was wrong with this picture?

I thought I knew, so I went to find Mert.

CHAPTER 29

I interrupted Mert while she was in the process of folding linens and setting them into a big cardboard box. "Got a sec? I need to tell you something. Could we go outside?"

She nodded impatiently and walked with me to the shady spot under the maple tree. Once there, she removed her hood and gloves. "Welcome to my office. Make it snappy. I got work to do. Ali Timmons stopped by again this morning to raise holy what-for. That there woman is sucking the energy right outta me. I mean, she shows up and cries and carries on and ever'thing comes to a screeching halt."

"Sorry about that. I'll get here early tomorrow. I don't have to work at the store. Took the day off."

Mert rubbed her eyes with a shaking hand. "It ain't about you. I know you're giving me whatever time you can. That Ali Timmons is dancing on my last nerve, that's all. She can't go more'n four hours at a stretch, calling me and talking up a storm."

"Why is she being such a pest?"

Mert shook her head and stared at the house, then toward the hulking green Dumpster that was nearly full with trash. Three blue recycling bins sat with their lids half-open. We'd filled them to overflowing. "I think it's about money."

"Isn't it always?"

"Pert near. Her hubby is outta work. Has been for some time. He's on disability, or so she says. Her mom should be paying for this, but Mrs. Timmons will have to go through some sort of legal wrangling to make that happen. And she feels guilty. She knew her mother was hoarding animals again. Even though they weren't speaking, a family friend had stopped by and seen all the kitties. But what could Ali do? If they'd list hoarding as a mental illness, maybe she coulda had power of attorney or something.

The way it is, Ali Timmons and her mother'd go 'round and 'round with her mom saying there weren't all that many cats—and the daughter tearing her hair out."

I sympathized. My mother lives in Arizona and I was grateful for the geographic distance between us. She and I didn't see eye-to-eye about much. There comes a point where you quit trying to find common ground and accept that you'll never agree. You revolve around each other like two magnets, kept at bay by a powerful force field. When you flipped those horseshoes around, an equally powerful attraction slammed the magnets together.

I doubted that I would ever be "free" of my mother. Not until one of us was in the grave. Even then, I suspected her words would linger in my head, like a stain you can't get out no matter how many times you bleached a garment.

Mert gestured toward a lawn chair. Grabbing us both a bottle of water, she said, "What's on your mind?"

"Something's wrong here."

Mert snickered so hard water squirted out of her nose. "You think? Let's see. We got a prime lot in Ladue with a tear-down on it. Tons of junk everywhere. Piles of cat excrement everywhere. More stacks of newspaper than the St. Louis County Library has. A dead woman in the freezer. Other'n that, this is just your everyday, ordinary cleaning job."

"Ha, ha, ha. Stop it and listen. Have you come across any cat food cans?"

"Nope."

"Or bags of food. Even any empty ones?"

"Nope."

"What was Marla feeding all those cats?"

Mert stared at me. "Who cares? That's the point, ain't it? She wasn't feeding them. They was fending for themselves."

"Think about it, Mert. There's not a can or a bag of chow in sight. In her notes for her scrapbook pages, she wrote that Devon was bringing her cat food. Sure, the cats were hungry and they were thin, but Marla didn't throw anything away. If there'd been a can or bag in the last year, we would have seen it. Most of the cats weren't that skinny. Not really. It wasn't like you could see their ribs."

"Maybe she fed them that hamburger you found in the refrigerator."

"In an exercise for our scrapbook class, she wrote about mixing the ground beef with kibble. But where's the kibble? Did you see any empty bags? I didn't. Maybe she mixed the beef with the rice I found in the pantry. But isn't that an expensive way to feed so many cats?"

"Beats me," Mert said. "I cain't afford beef more than twice a week. Who knows? Maybe it ain't beef. Maybe it's venison and a hunter supplies her with it. That way she don't have to pay nothing. In fact, she'd be doing a public service. We got eighty deer per square mile in St. Louis County. That's ridiculous. It's four times the recommended number by wildlife specialists. Four times!"

"Right." I got comfortable in my chair and prepared myself for Mert's rant. This was a soapbox she climbed on regularly.

"Last year, a deer ran into a woman in a parking lot. I ain't talking about the animal running into her car. He ran into her person! Knocked her six ways to Sunday. The folks in a nearby office thought there'd been an automobile accident, 'cause the force of the impact was so hard."

"Uh-huh." I didn't need to say more, because she was off and running.

"Last year there were 3,420 deer strikes, that's cars hitting deer on our roads. Two people died from the collisions. And some of them so-called experts in the county think they oughta spend our hard-earned money for sterilization of them critters! Yeah, right. Drag some poor doe off into the bushes and do a major operation on her in the wild? Are they insane?"

"Sort of," I said. Mert was passionate about animals, but she also had tons of common sense. Too bad so many lawmakers seemed shortchanged in that department.

"It ain't fair to the deer! They cain't survive in such numbers! They ain't got nothin' to eat, and they're getting hurt by cars and dragging their sorry carcasses off the road to die in misery. I'd rather take a bullet to the head than to bleed to death slowly or be attacked by predators."

"Predators?"

"Coyotes. Rats. Whatever."

Most people don't realize it, but St. Louis has a small population of wild coyotes. Rats? Well, despite all the cats, Marla's house was an example of a haven for the large rodents. They probably nested in the attic. Maybe they tunneled through crawl spaces. Whatever means they used to get around, they still managed to live, thrive, and multiply in Marla's house.

Mert was still talking. "Do you realize that one of them nearby municipalities actually tried to tag and relocate their deer population? Twenty percent of those poor critters died within a month of what they call 'capture myopathy,' which means they slowly wasted away until scavengers got 'em."

She took a breath, but continued, "Meanwhile there's an organization call Hunters Feeding the Hungry. They estimate that every carcass yields about forty pounds of ground venison. That's a humane response to overpopulation, and a smart one, 'cause hungry people can fill their bellies."

I wanted to change the subject. "Have you heard anything new about Marla? An update on her condition?"

"No, and I ain't hopeful, neither. When Ali Timmons talked to me right before you got here, she said that unless her mother makes a miraculous, saints-be-praised recovery—and I doubt that'll happen—they're expecting the worse. That girl seemed almost gleeful. Made my stomach turn."

Mine too. I couldn't imagine Anya being eager for me to die.

"On that cheerful note, ready to go back to work? I want this job over and the money in my pocket." Mert tossed her empty water bottle into a low recycling bin. I did the same.

We walked back to the house, wordlessly, lost in our thoughts about Marla Lever and her sad situation.

CHAPTER 30

Around two, a silver Toyota SUV pulled up. A nicely dressed man wearing a blue sports coat and a striped silk tie hopped out of the Avalon and started toward us. As he walked, he straightened his tie self-consciously, before adjusting his cuffs. There was an air of prissiness about him, a sense that he liked everything just so.

We were finishing up our mandatory water break under the maple tree where the shade felt delicious. Dirt smudges marred our faces, and to put it kindly, we stunk to high heavens. The heat intensified the natural odor of our sweat, but that had combined with the stench of the garbage we hauled out to create a truly odiferous perfume of sorts.

The man walked over to Mert, who had crossed the lawn to meet him halfway. He hoisted his pants in that manly (ha!) way some guys have. "I'm Devon Timmons."

"I'm Mert Chambers." She extended her hand for a shake. "Your wife hired me to clean out her mother's house. This is my crew."

Mert's hand was clean. I know that because I saw her wash it. But Devon Timmons took two fingers of hers as though he were picking up a dead fish. His face broadcast his disgust. Mert's shoulders sagged a little as she stepped away from him, accepting his distaste.

My turn to rant: There are three kinds of male handshaking techniques. One is to squeeze your hand hard, driving your rings into your skin so that they hurt like crazy. The second is to touch you as if your flesh was packed with cooties, and that's downright insulting. The third is the proper way, which is to grasp a hand with no more and no less pressure than one might use to pick up a glass of water.

I knew that Mert often encountered derision because of her

job. "Cleaning lady," people would repeat with a look of superiority. They were always surprised to learn that she held a degree in history from Southern Missouri. Over the years, she has made a very good living from her cleaning business. As far as I know, she's never been unemployed, whereas Devon Timmons didn't have a job. At least, his wife had said he didn't, claiming he was on disability. Maybe he was. To the casual observer (that would be me), he didn't look like he had any physical problems, unless you count a bad attitude.

Everything about him suggested he found Mert to be his inferior.

Even if the situation had been different, even if he was the President of the United States of America, Devon Timmons should have treated Mert with respect. She deserved it. We all do.

Johnny walked up behind his sister, in a gesture of solidarity. After years in prison, he had a way of sizing up a situation, a survival instinct. Noting the change in Mert's posture, Johnny also changed his stance. I wouldn't say he was threatening, a hair short of that, but he definitely gathered himself into a command posture that announced, "I don't take any guff from anyone."

"Well." Timmons looked us over, sniffed the air with a sneer of his lip, and found us wanting. "Good to have you here. Big job, huh? Nasty. I don't envy you."

I bet he didn't. I doubted that this man had worked a day of physical labor in his life.

"How may I help you, Mr. Timmons?" Mert's voice was cool, professional, and her enunciation clean and crisp. All her Missouri-isms disappeared.

"You can't help me." The tone suggested he was fully aware of the double-meaning. "I dropped by to pick up my lawn mower and a few other tools."

Mert nodded. "I see. Unfortunately, I can't allow that."

"Come again? What do you mean, you can't allow that?"

"Mrs. Timmons hired me. I am responsible to her for everything on this property. If she tells me you can take your tools, that's fine, but otherwise, I can't allow it."

"That's...that's..." and he cursed. "Look, I don't have time to call Ali about every little thing I do. I'm a busy man."

"Busy" and "unemployed" usually don't appear in the same sentence. Maybe he didn't realize that.

"I am sorry for the inconvenience." Mert actually sounded regretful.

"That's the point, isn't it? You shouldn't cause me any inconvenience. You were hired to work for us, not cause problems."

Oh, doggies. The gloves had come off and the smacking around had begun.

"I came to get my things," Devon Timmons said, "and I plan to do exactly that. Marla told me I could have her father's tools."

To punctuate his comment, he stamped his foot. It sure looks silly when a grown man does it.

"Mr. Timmons, sir, I'd hate to have to press the point. Honest I would. But I'll call the authorities if you persist," Mert said in an unnaturally calm voice.

"You try that. You just try that." Devon Timmons tried to push his way past Mert, but Trudy and I stepped into place right next to Johnny. The three of us made a protective wall with our bodies, effectively blocking Devon's route up the sidewalk. We guessed, and he confirmed, that he was too much of a wuss to step into the tall grasses.

I pulled out my cell phone and held it up to make it obvious.

"Mert? You want me to make the call?"

Devon Timmons cursed but took a step backwards and pointed at me. "What's your name?"

"Kiki Lowenstein." I returned his stare. I was not about to back down.

"You're good at calling the authorities, aren't you? You're the busybody who called the cops originally. I recognize your name. Stuck your nose where it didn't belong. Well, you haven't heard the last of me." Devon pointed a finger at me, mimicked holding a gun, and pretended to shoot me.

"You are threatening Police Chief Robbie Holmes' stepdaughter," Johnny said, exaggerating my status a little since the police chief and my mother-in-law were only going steady, or whatever you call it when you're both creeping up on sixty years of age.

"Really? Color me scared." Devon flipped a hand in the air.

"Just saying." Johnny added a shrug. "You ought to know who you're dealing with."

"She'll learn who she's dealing with." He pointed to me and then went down the line. "I'm not done with her or her or her or you, tough guy."

Devon hopped into his car and threw it in reverse with wheels spinning and tossing up grass and rocks. From my spot in the yard, I could clearly see that he'd lifted one side of his upper lip in an ugly snarl. His car was traveling backward far too fast to be safe. He was headed for Mert's candy apple red Chevy S10. I closed my eyes in expectation of a loud crash. It never came.

When I opened them, he was barreling down the street, going easily 30 mph over the speed limit.

"Show's over, folks," said Mert. "Back to work.

CHAPTER 31

By three o'clock, we were staggering around from the effects of the heat and general exhaustion. Every muscle in my body screamed in protest.

Mert whistled us to the gathering spot.

Taking off our masks and helmets was such a treat. There wasn't much of a breeze, but the maple leaves sheltered us from the sun. My hair was soaked with perspiration and glued to my head. Even Trudy suffered from an advanced case of hood-hair. Her ponytail was dripping wet with perspiration. Johnny's forehead was dotted with sweat, and Mert couldn't have been more tuckered out. Her shoulders slumped and her head drooped. We opened our Tyvek suits so we could cool down. If you ignored the white jumpers, we looked like a trio who'd entered a wet tee shirt contest…and lost.

"Let's take a minute to recap where we are," Mert said wearily.

Trudy had been tasked with hanging all Marla's clothes in wardrobe boxes to be taken to a laundry facility. Every piece of fabric in the house stunk of cat pee. After consulting with Mert, who then called Ali, Trudy tossed all Marla's shoes into boxes. The footwear would have to be burned because most of it had been used as litter boxes. After completing that particular chore, Trudy had worked steadily all afternoon to sort through a huge stack of jewelry boxes.

"I filled this bag with junk like plastic bangles," said Trudy. "I know you'll want to show Mrs. Timmons, but I did try to sort the obvious garbage from pieces that might have value."

Johnny had been assigned the garage. Sagging cardboard boxes had been stacked high around Marla's car, and each of these was stuffed to the brim with rags, tools, pieces of wood, and so on. All of that had to be sorted. Who knew what might be sitting at the bottom of a box? One by one, he'd removed them and gone through the contents. He was about a third of the way done.

Mert had emptied a sideboard, taking her time wrapping and boxing up glasses, dishes, bowls, and cutlery. "There was Spode china in there and cut glass, so I took extra care packing it up. I cain't tell if it's worth anything, but it looked like nice dinnerware."

I'd been assigned the task of boxing up the pots and pans, mixing bowls, and kitchen utensils. The kitchen was now empty.

"We're making progress. Slow and steady," Mert said.

A bronze Jeep pulled up to the curb in front of the house.

The man who climbed out was obviously Ali Timmons' twin, Allen Lever. No question about it. With a change of hairstyle and a shave, he could have taken her place, except that he was smaller than his sister. But whereas Ali exuded self-righteous authority, Allen could have made a guest appearance as the nerd in an episode of *The Office*, thanks to his thick glasses, lace-up shoes, and the plastic pen protector in the top pocket of his polyester shirt. He stood with his hands on the hips of his polyester pants as he surveyed the Dumpster, recycling bins, and trash bags. With a shake of his head, he came closer to us, giving a small tug on his collar to let a little air in.

"Which of you is Mert Chambers?"

Mert stepped forward and introduced herself.

"I thought I'd poke around. See if Mom kept my old vinyl records."

"I am sorry, sir, but I cain't allow that." For the second time that day, Mert explained her responsibility to Ali Timmons.

"I've got my own key to Mom's house."

"Your sister changed the locks," Mert said quietly. "Did that first thing after your mom was taken to the hospital, and the police checked out the premises."

"Shoot." He pinched the bridge of his nose. "Ali thinks of everything, doesn't she?"

None of us responded. What could we say?

Trudy, however, shifted her weight and gave her hair a toss in a totally "come hither" way. Considering how wet it was, the gesture seemed ridiculous. For the first time, I took a long hard look at her. Not only had she shrugged off the top of her Tyvek jumpsuit, but she'd obviously also decided to go braless today. Wooo-ee, but Allen Lever was getting an eye full.

"Mr. Lever, sir, I suggest you call your sister. If she gives me permission, you can have access," Mert said.

"What are you doing with the stuff you find?" Tearing his eyes away from Trudy, Allen shoved one hand into his pants pocket and jingled change. "I mean, I assume you're sifting through all this. There might be a few nuggets of gold in that trash."

"This here's called a truck deck." Mert slapped the back of her truck. "Fits under my truck bed liner. See them locks? That's how I'm protecting anything that looks like it might be of value."

She went on to explain how she logged and took photos of anything that could possibly be high-dollar. These items were tucked inside the storage drawers that slid under the deck of her truck bed. Only Mert knew the combinations to the padlocks. She even offered to show him proof that she was insured, but Allen waved that away.

"Granddad owned a bunch of woodworking tools that I'd like to have," said Allen, as he pulled his keys out of his pocket. He began tossing them in the air and catching them repeatedly. "My grandfather and a couple of his friends did sculptures out of wood. In fact, there might be a few of them still left in the garage. If there are, I want them."

"I haven't come across those yet. Are they clear in the back of the garage?" Johnny asked. "I'm only a third of the way along."

"They could be," Allen said.

"I'll keep an eye out for them," Johnny said.

You could tell that Allen Lever wanted to voice a protest, but after a short stare-down he finally nodded.

"How is your mother?" Mert asked.

Allen wiped a bead of perspiration from his forehead.

"Here." Trudy trotted over and offered the man a bottle of water.

"Thanks." He took the bottle. "It doesn't look good. I guess all we can do is pray. She's been off her nut for years. We cut off contact, trying to force her to get help. She told me she was seeing someone, a psychologist, but I'm not sure I believe that. I wasn't supposed to be in contact with her—Ali said if we both backed off maybe she'd come around—but I still called her now and again. I'd come by once in a blue moon and take her to lunch. Bring her bags of cat food and kitty litter. Try to talk sense into her. I mean, Ali said we needed to take a stand, but...."

"She was still your mother," Mert filled in for him.

So he was the initial "A" who'd brought Marla the cat food.

"You poor baby," said Trudy, batting her lashes. "You must be heartbroken."

I rolled my eyes at Johnny, and he fought a snicker.

"You know it, but Ali is my big sister — she's the oldest by five minutes – she kept telling me to stay away." He shoved his hands and the keys deep in his pockets. "Now this. Maybe if I hadn't listened to Ali, I could have gotten through to Mom. At least she might have called me about the A/C going out. It's a good thing someone found her before it was too late."

"The person to thank is right there," said Mert, pointing a finger in my direction.

"I'm Kiki Lowenstein." I stepped forward. Allen stared at me as if trying to place my name. "Your mother frequented the scrapbook store where I work. She seemed like a nice person.

I'm keeping her in my prayers."

"Look, I'm grateful that you called an ambulance, but why'd you have to get the cops involved?"

I opened my mouth to explain that I hadn't called the cops, that they came in response to my 911 call, but he wasn't finished.

"You say you know Mom. Well, then you have to know that Mom wouldn't hurt a fly. Literally. That's how she got into this mess. She never met an animal she didn't love. A few of those cats were wild and would just as soon attack you as look at you, but Mom couldn't stand the idea of them being homeless. The idea of her killing someone and stuffing that woman in her freezer, well, that's just crazy! Thanks to you, the cops think she's a killer!"

He'd wound himself up. With each word, his face got redder and redder. He finished his water and tossed the empty bottle on the ground. The message was clear: we were supposed to pick up after him.

"Your brother-in-law stopped by earlier," Mert said, in an attempt to change the subject. With a minimum of fuss, she picked up the empty plastic bottle.

"Yeah, great. Just great. What did good old Devon want?"

"Same as you."

"Except he doesn't have any right to any of this. I do. Especially my granddad's tools."

"I also explained to him that he needed to call Mrs. Timmons. If she gives me a release, I'll follow her instructions. Just so you know, I'm being consistent."

"Consistent but not fair! Part of this is mine," Allen said as his face turned redder and redder. "My sister had no right to hire you without my consent. She can't keep me off this property or away from Mom's stuff."

Mert sighed. "That's something for you to take up with her."

"Believe me, I will. I'm not going to beg Ali for anything. Do you hear me? Everything on this property is mine as much as hers. She had no right to hire you! None!"

Mert stuck to her message. "I understand, and I am sorry, but you'll have to take it up with your sister."

"Believe me, I will."

He turned on his heel and stomped off toward his car. But when he reached the handle of his Jeep, he stopped and yelled, "When I come back, I plan to kick you all off her property. Including you, scrapbook girl. What's your name? Lowenstein? Huh? Yeah, that's it. I won't forget you! None of this would have happened if you hadn't gone and called the cops."

CHAPTER 32

Allen Lever jumped into his car and keyed the engine, but before he could put the Jeep in gear, we heard a shout.

"Allen! Allen, wait!"

Our heads swiveled toward the sound, as a man stepped out of the tall grasses at the rear of Marla's yard. Picking his way carefully through the weeds, he moved toward us, but he didn't give us a second glance. He was totally focused on Allen Lever.

"Allen, wait up!"

Rolling down his window and shielding his eyes with his hand, Allen Lever scanned the yard. Because he was facing the sun, he squinted. "Fred? That you?"

"In the flesh." The interloper stalked right past us without acknowledging our presence. As he passed by, I noticed a hint of gray in his buzz-cut hair. Otherwise, I didn't get a good look at Fred, because he made a beeline toward Allen Lever.

The two men exchanged a manly hug, more like a shoulder bump than a real embrace. As we watched they talked in low tones, obviously keeping their conversation a secret. The men couldn't have been more different. The newcomer reminded me of a bantam rooster, overtly showy and crowing about his manhood. I'd guess he was in his late fifties. His red knit shirt was open at the neck so that a gold chain could sparkle in the sunlight. A pinky ring with a large stone winked from his little finger.

My fellow cleaners and I didn't move. We all suspected that this Fred, or whatever his name was, would give Mert more grief about the cleaning process. Sure enough, the men finished talking, and Fred waited for Allen to pull away. Then he walked toward us with a stiff-legged gait.

"You have to forgive Allen," said the newcomer as he watched Marla Lever's son drive away. "I heard him raise his voice to you, but that's not like him. He's obviously distressed. He's usually very calm under pressure. A great guy. Smart as a whip."

"I'm Mert Chambers." My friend extended her hand yet again.

"Fred Ernest," he introduced himself and grabbed her hand. I could tell from the wince, he squeezed it hard. "It's a real shame about Mrs. Lever, isn't it? Who would have guessed? A cat hoarder and a murderer living in a nice neighborhood like this. Boggles the mind, doesn't it?"

He raised his hand to adjust his collar. The motion sent off a wave of expensive men's cologne.

Mert nodded. "The jury is still out on whether she had anything to do with the corpse in her freezer."

"Looks pretty bad for poor Marla, doesn't it? Beating someone to death with a baseball bat. That's amazing." Fred extended his hand to each of us in turn, asking our names, and passing out business cards. I was glad I didn't wear rings anymore because his handshake would have been painful.

"You live next-door?" Mert glanced back the way that Fred had come through the weeds.

"For more than a decade and a half now. I've tried to be a good neighbor, honestly I have. After Marla's husband walked out on her, I told her I'd do whatever I could to help out. I cleaned her driveway in the winter, offered to mow her lawn, and drove her to the store when her car quit working. I did my best to be a good role model for Allen, too. Took him to ball games. You know the drill. Guy stuff. Poor kid. Totally henpecked with a mom and a sister who was frankly overbearing. But as for Marla, Lord knows I encouraged her to clean the place up. Did everything I could. She'd get the place under control for about a month and wham! Back to this. Disgusting, isn't it?"

"You put up with all her cats?" asked Trudy. She batted her

lashes and tugged the scrunchy from her ponytail. When her hair was free, she shook it out, letting the damp locks drape over her shoulders.

Personally, I thought her behavior was a bit much. I didn't think Fred was at all attractive, but I'm picky like that. Maybe too picky. I pushed aside thoughts of Detweiler.

"The cats didn't bother me. Not really. I have too much on my plate. I own my own business, and I keep crazy hours. Phone calls all the time. Meetings with clients. Busy, busy, busy," he said as he hoisted his pants.

"Wow, and this is your company?" asked Trudy, tapping the business card. Again she began with the hair flipping.

"Right. Computer installations. Huge deals. Megabucks."

I covered my mouth rather than laugh out loud. I hate when people brag about money. It's so unseemly. If you have it, why shout about it? Surely we'll figure it out on our own.

"How long you think you're going to be working here?" asked Fred.

"Until the job is done," Mert said.

"Allen told me that one of you stumbled into this mess?"

"I did," I said.

"Thank goodness you did. Probably saved Marla's life. How'd that happen?"

"We were supposed to have a scrapbooking party here."

He affected a thoughtful posture, tapping his cheek with his index finger. "That's right. Marla mentioned it to me. As you can see, her house would not have been the ideal place for a get-together. Not at all."

None of us responded.

"Okay." He slapped his hands together. "I didn't mean to interrupt. This is great because Marla's mess hurts all of our property values. Especially mine. Everything in my house is top-of-the-line. Custom built. Spent a fortune on landscaping. You should see my exotic orchids."

Uh, no thanks, I thought.

"I hope we'll be through by the end of this week," Mert said.

"If I can help you in any way, let me know." With that, he started to walk away, but he turned to ask, "By the way, what's the update on Marla's condition? I forgot to ask Allen. Didn't want to upset him. I could call Ali, of course."

"We've been told Marla is in a bad way," said Mert. "That's all I know."

"But do they expect her to come out of it?" The man sounded truly concerned. "With her wits about her?"

"I couldn't say." Mert shook her head sadly.

CHAPTER 33

"I've almost got that full." With a jerk of my head, I indicated to Mert that we'd need a second recycling container for newspapers. Four o'clock and the muscles in my back had already seized up. Did I know how to have a good time or what?

I grabbed a bottle of cold water and chased down two Advils. Planting my knuckles in my lower back, I did the best I could to give myself relief.

"Johnny?" Mert called to her brother. "Check out the garage and see if there's anything in there we can use temporarily. Drag stuff out if you need to. We'll need a path."

"Yes, ma'am." He wandered off. In a few minutes he was back. "You got to see this."

We dutifully followed Johnny into the garage, although we couldn't go very far. Marla's car took up most of the space.

"This here car's a cream puff," said Johnny, in an admiring tone. I didn't need a look-see, because I'd seen Marla's car before. The gold Impala had a cream leather roof and matching interior. Unlike the rest of everything that Marla owned, the car was spotless. Johnny carefully opened a door and reached in the glove compartment. "All the service records are here. Looks like she took fantastic care of this beast. Low mileage, too."

After giving the car a few more lustful glances, Johnny added, "But that ain't all. You'll have to walk sideways, but you can get through to the back now. I've cleared a path."

I dutifully followed my friends deeper into the building.

"Allen was right. See these? Totems!" His arm swept wide and he stepped back. A bear, a sun, a bald eagle, and a pond lily stared out of a tree trunk. All had been carved crudely, as if the artist had started and been called away. Behind that totem stood other large pieces of uncut wood, looking like telephone poles, but more roughly hewn.

"Dusty as all get out," said Mert, running a finger over the statue. "Did you find the tools?"

"Yeah." Johnny pointed to another area of the garage, but my eyes were struggling to adjust. "Chainsaws, hacksaws, keyhole saws, chisels, chains of all sizes, a skid, and a wood chipper. Makes sense, don't it? The old man musta cut down the trees himself. Dragged them here. Worked on them."

"Look at that." Trudy pushed past us.

After squinting, I saw it, a large pulley attached to a support beam. From the pulley dangled a short length of chain that split into two shorter lengths connected to a metal bar with hooks on each end.

"This here's a hoist. A hunter could dress a deer with that." As Johnny talked, his hand reached for the wall behind him. A flick, a sizzle, and a fluorescent light hummed to life.

"Yuck," squealed Trudy. "Deer hooves. Is that gross or what?" I heard her, but I couldn't take my eyes off the pattern of blood that had seeped into the concrete floor and spattered the drywall behind the hook.

"Maybe Allen or Devon are members of that group. Hunters for the Hungry, or whatever you called them, Mert." I was trying to be funny, but my voice cracked. All that dried blood was too much for me.

"I guess we've found the source of the venison." Mert nodded. "One more mess to clean up, huh? Okay, showtime's over. Johnny, did you find a recycling bin we can use?"

"No, Sis."

"How about if I ask Mr. Ernest if we can borrow a recycling bin from him?" Trudy bounced on her toes. "That'll hold us for a while. I need a break anyway. I love slasher movies but this makes me want to toss my cookies."

"Go ask him," said Mert. "I need to talk to Ali Timmons. While none of this wooden pole mess appeals to me, a person might call it art. What do you think, Kiki?"

I was relieved to turn my attention to the carvings. "I don't know much about it, but I do recall that the Osage Indians populated this area. The bald eagle was one of their favorite images. You don't want to mess with any of those without making sure you know what you're doing. Who knows? That ugly chunk of wood might be worth a fortune."

Not to me.

Leaving Johnny to work around the totem, Mert and I walked out of the garage and into the sunshine. Over at the coolers, we gulped our fill of cold water. Neither of us spoke for a long, long while. Finally, she said, "I'm sorry for dragging you into this."

"Is that how it happened? I thought it was the other way around."

"Iff'n so, you owe me a giant-sized apology." We both laughed, although the sound of our guffaws was slightly strained.

Trudy came back with a blue bin in tow and a big grin on her face. "You should see that guy's place. It's like, like, the Playboy mansion. His landscaping is fabulous. His lawn looks like a golf course!"

"Really?" I was only half-listening.

"Flowers blooming everywhere. All sorts of neat high-tech stuff."

I'd just pulled my gloves back on to start hauling more newspapers when Devon Timmons pulled up in the drive again.

"I've told Ali I'm going to list this place. I've got a real estate agent who'll be here this Friday. You need to be done," he said as he planted his fists on his hips. "I want all this junk out of here."

"We're doing our best, Mr. Timmons," Mert said. "I hadn't heard about your deadline. Your wife didn't share that with me."

Although her words were perfectly conciliatory, there was an edge to her tone. An edge that Devon Timmons wasn't about to ignore. He got right in Mert's face and shook his index finger.

"Now you listen to me. I'm the boss of your boss. Get it? And I plan to tear this house down and build a place worth a fortune on this lot. This'll be a big real estate deal. In fact, I might even be able to put up two houses here. I'll know for sure soon enough. You aren't going to ruin this for me, understand?"

Johnny came out from where he'd been working in the garage. In one hand was a tire iron. "I suggest you back off Mr. Timmons."

Mert moved her body to put a barrier between her brother and Devon Timmons. "Mr. Timmons, sir, I haven't heard from your wife about what she wants to do. I'd appreciate it if you'd have her call me. I'm not disputing your authority. I jest need everything to be crystal clear."

"I'll tell you what's crystal clear," he said, but he did take a step backwards and he didn't lock eyes with Johnny. "My mother-in-law isn't coming out of her coma. She's brain dead. We got the word an hour ago. So Ali's got power of attorney. My wife will do what I tell her to. You can take that to the bank."

"Excuse me, sir, but I still have Marla's photos at my store. How should I get them to your wife? Is she coming by?"

In retrospect, I should have kept my mouth shut. I could have gotten Ali's address from Mert. I was thinking out loud rather than buttoning my lip. As the kids say, "My bad."

"You again? I want you off this property and I want you to leave right now. I plan to sit here in my car with the A/C running until I see you go."

CHAPTER 34

Why on earth were these people blaming me for Marla's problems? In my little pea brain, I thought they should be thanking me for finding her and getting her out alive!

"Don't let him bother you," said Mert, putting an arm around my shoulder. The move was brief because it was too hot for human contact. "They're all looking for somebody to point the finger at, and you're an easy target. I put in a call to Ali Timmons, and she's on her way here in person to calm down her husband. I gave her our condolences. She still seems to think there's hope for her mother, but she ain't being honest with herself."

"I am so sorry, Mert. I should have waited and asked you about how to return Marla's stuff. I jumped the gun." I shook my head. "It's this heat. It's getting to me."

"You're hyper-responsible when it comes to people's pictures. I know that. But yeah, I wished you'd kept your yapper shut."

We stood under the maple tree, letting the cool breeze play over our wet skin. Mert had sent Johnny to buy more water for us. Trudy had cheerfully gone with.

"Good thinking on your part getting your brother out of here," I said. The sight of him holding that tire iron had put a scare into me. What was he capable of? I didn't want to know.

But Mert read my mind. "When Johnny was locked up in Petosi, he learned never to back down. I can understand that. I mean, in prison that was smart 'cause if you show fear, you're doomed. But out here, it's not smart. I need to talk with him about being such an alpha male."

"Did you notice how quickly Trudy jumped in the truck with him?" I was trying to lighten the mood. Devon Timmons still glowered at us from his silver Toyota. I could feel the heat of his glare as Mert and I wiped our bare skin with damp washcloths.

"That brother of mine's always been a hit with the ladies. As for Trudy, let's just say the elastic on her panties is stretched out from pulling them off so often, okay?"

I laughed at that. The release felt great.

"And nosy? That woman! I can't let her clean the bathrooms when she comes with me on a job, 'cause she snoops around and looks at all the pill containers and such."

We both snickered at Trudy's insatiable curiosity. Mert sighed. "Speaking of my brother, he's got his eye on you. Don't think I haven't noticed."

I couldn't think of anything appropriate to say, so I kept my mouth shut. However, Mert wasn't done talking. "I know you still have the hots for that there detective, and I heard your mother-in-law is pushing that Ben Novak on you. But I just wanted you to know, Johnny's a good man with a good heart. He's had a few hard knocks, but he'll make someone a loving husband. Someday."

She was probably right, but I couldn't see myself with him. Yes, Johnny was exciting, but when I was brutally honest with myself, I wanted more out of life than he could give me. Even if I fell in love with him, I doubted that I could ever be wholly content with the life we would make together.

If I'd learned nothing from my first marriage except for one thing, it was this: A marriage can't be successful unless the spouses are pulling in the same direction. They can have different backgrounds, experiences, and outlooks, but they have to agree on their goals—and on the sort of lifestyle they want. Sure, I liked backyard barbecues and country music, but I also wanted to dress up, eat at a fancy restaurant, and hear the symphony. To make my world complete, I needed a man who was comfortable at both ends of the cultural spectrum.

My musings were interrupted with a squeal of tires. Ali

Timmons' car came racing around the corner. Her husband got out of his Toyota. I couldn't hear their conversation, but it must have been a doozy because he was red in the face and shouting obscenities before he hopped back in his car and drove off.

"Golly," I said, as he spun rubber on the hot pavement. "All three of them should have been race car drivers."

"Nope," Mert said. "Takes a cool head to drive a hot car on a fast track. None of those dopes could manage it."

I stood off to one side while Mert talked to Ali Timmons. The confab didn't last long. They looked like they were done talking when Johnny and Trudy returned and climbed out of Mert's truck. The three of us worked to restock the ice chest with bottles of water. Out of the corner of my eyes, I saw Mert wave goodbye to Ali Timmons.

My friend joined us under the maple tree.

"Mrs. Timmons would like us to get this done by Friday. She's got an expert in aboriginal art coming by on Saturday to look at the totem poles. I told her I didn't know if we could get a wide path cleared through the garage to haul them out. Can we, Johnny?"

"Don't need one. You can get through the back door."

"What back door?"

"Didn't I show it to you, Sis? I found it earlier, but it was blocked from the inside. A trellis is propped against it on the outside so's you couldn't see it. But them hinges have been oiled recently. Shouldn't be a problem getting in and out, as long as Mrs. Timmons comes in from the back."

"Thank the Lord for small favors. I thought we'd have most of the junk cleared out, but this is taking longer than I expected. Ali Timmons started whining because she jest promised her hubby he could bring in a hot-shot real estate agent he was bragging on. We compromised with that agent coming over this Friday afternoon. Like he said, they're hoping they can build two houses on this one lot. They got a local agent who can tell them if that's gonna work. It's bigger than a lot of other plots in this neighborhood, so there's a chance that might work."

"That would mean a lot of money," I said.

"But Marla has to die first, and as Ali Timmons pointed out, she's not dead yet," said Mert. "Can you imagine? Having your family eager to see you go so they can get their mitts on your worldly goods? Shoot fire, I'd rather be poor. Rather have nothing of value. What a miserable excuse for kin folk."

"Maybe that's why Marla loved those cats."

"That's why mothers eat their young," Mert said. "Nine months of labor, six hours of pain, and misery ever after."

CHAPTER 35

Monday evening...

On the way home from Marla's, I stopped by Pasta House, a local chain, and picked up several dishes that I knew Anya, Rebekkah, and I would enjoy. Since I had a little extra cash coming in, I splurged and bought a couple of their stuffed artichokes. A little green dough buys a lot of pasta dough at Pasta House, and I struggled to my car with a shopping bag full of food. The spicy Italian dressing that they use on their salads is a house specialty. My mouth watered with anticipation as I imagined chomping into those cool, crunchy bits of lettuce, red onion, pimentos, and artichoke hearts. Their freshly baked miniature bread loaves beckoned me, but I knew better than to even indulge myself by pinching off the end of one.

If I did, I wouldn't stop. However, the smell of the yeast was intoxicating. Finally, while sitting at a red light, I broke down, reached deep in the bag, and located a warm loaf and crammed it into my mouth, whole.

Practicing restraint isn't all it's cracked up to be.

At another stoplight, I phoned Rebekkah and asked her to set the table. She said she would be happy to. That put a smile on my face.

Despite the yucky work conditions I'd endured, this was shaping up to be a good day. Fortunately, I was scheduled at the store the next day. That meant I'd get a well-deserved break from the heat and the filth.

As soon as I walked through the back door, I handed the paper shopping bag full of food to Rebekkah. "I'm so gross. I really, really need a shower, if you don't mind."

She didn't. She could see what a mess I was.

Standing under the hot water, I soaped myself repeatedly, trying to wash away any traces of Marla Lever's house of horrors. I was patting myself dry when I heard voices outside the bathroom door. My mother-in-law's distinctively precise enunciation has a tendency to carry. Wrapping a towel around my head, I quickly threw on a pair of drawstring pants and a tee shirt to make myself presentable.

"Honestly, Kiki, how on earth do you get involved in these awful situations?" asked Sheila as I stepped out of the bathroom and into the hallway.

As usual her makeup was perfectly applied, and her hair freshly styled. Today she wore nicely tailored slacks in a lovely shade of blue, nearly royal but more navy. Her chiffon blouse picked up that color and added a jade green. On her feet were strappy sandals in the same shade of jade. At least I hadn't walked out of my bathroom naked.

"Pardon?" I decided to play dumb. "What awful situation?"

"Robbie told me that you're the one who alerted the police to the condition of Marla Lever's house. He says you were actually there, on the scene. On her doorstep! That you went inside!"

"Yup."

"Please speak like an educated person and not a hillbilly."

"Yes, ma'am. I went inside. I am the responsible party. Or the irresponsible party, depending on your viewpoint."

"What on earth possessed you? I thought that place had been condemned. I can't imagine stepping foot inside. That must have been ghastly."

I covered my mouth with the towel I was using on my hair so she wouldn't see my smile. Ghastly? Sheila had a wide vocabulary and wasn't afraid to use it.

"It wasn't staged for an Architectural Digest photo shoot, that's for sure."

Sheila blocked my way. I couldn't get past her to go to my kitchen. All I could do was sniff the food and salivate.

"I do hope you aren't planning to return there. Not under any circumstances. Think of the germs you came in contact with. The vermin. Why, you might have brought home something contagious like head lice!"

"I hope not."

"She brought home a cat, Gran," said my daughter. Anya slipped her arms around her grandmother's waist and stared up at her. Both women had denim blue eyes and thin builds. Anya looked more like Sheila than she did like me. Together they made a stunning pair.

Despite my mother-in-law's obsession with cleanliness and propriety, she adored my daughter from day one. No amount of baby spit up or disgusting diapers could dissuade Sheila from spending time with her grandchild. Once when Anya had a stomach virus, she upchucked all over a beautiful silk blouse that Sheila was wearing. Although a tiny "eeek!" escaped my mother-in-law's lips, she didn't carry on about how my baby had clearly ruined an expensive garment. Instead, she handed Anya to me, excused herself, and changed into another blouse.

I admired that about Sheila. She certainly had her priorities in the right place when it came to Anya.

"Your mother brought you a what? A cat? From that awful, horrible, disgusting—"

"A kitten. A survivor," I broke in. "Anya, why don't you introduce your grandmother to Martin?"

I wasn't sure how Sheila felt about cats. I'd only recently learned she actually liked dogs. Small dogs, that is. As Sheila pouted there in my hallway, I figured this should prove interesting. Anya disappeared and came back cuddling Martin.

"My, my. He's a handsome fellow." Sheila held out her arms and took the kitten. Holding him close to her face, she cooed, "Oh, listen to him purr."

I have to admit: Sheila never failed to amaze me. Just about the time I thought she'd given the word "insufferable" a new twist, she did something entirely out of character. Beneath that iceberg exterior there had to be a heart. Somewhere. Even if it was flash-frozen.

"Rebekkah, isn't he adorable?" Sheila walked off toward my tiny living room and left me trailing behind. She knew Rebekkah because she knew Dodie. Our families attended the same temple.

"He is so, so cute." Rebekkah stood there, stroking Martin's head with her thick fingers.

"Well, I'm going to turn this little fellow over to you," Sheila said reluctantly, handing Martin back to Anya. "Robbie is taking me to dinner tonight and I promised I wouldn't be late. What are your plans for tomorrow, Anya darling?"

"Mom's making me go to that horrible summer camp. I get out at four."

"How about if I come and pick you up? I wanted to take you to Frontenac. We need to look for school clothes."

Bless her. Thanks to Sheila my daughter attended the Charles and Anne Lindbergh Academy, known locally as CALA. Being a student there was a family tradition, and since the education was top-notch I couldn't complain. However, on account of my husband's untimely demise, I couldn't dress Anya in the sort of clothes most of the students wore. Nor could I afford the yearly "gift" expected of all families. That's where Sheila stepped up to the plate. She made sure that Anya fit in with her fellow students.

"Is that all right with you, Kiki?" Sheila asked. "Picking up Anya and taking her shopping?"

And of course, I said yes.

"By the way," Sheila added, "Leah Novak and I are trying to find a suitable date for our families to have dinner together. Please tell me that you'll be done with this horrible part-time job, cleaning that disgusting house in Ladue, sooner rather than later? I'd really rather not have that mess become a topic of conversation at the dinner table."

Good old Sheila. It didn't matter that one woman was dead

and another had one foot in the grave. My mother-in-law had her priorities, and by golly, a pleasant conversation over dinner was right up there at the top of the list.

But before I could reassure her that the job was coming to a speedy conclusion, she raised an eyebrow and added, "A man like Ben won't stay single for long. You need to snap him up, Kiki. Mark my words."

Fortunately, Sheila didn't expect a reply.

CHAPTER 36

After Sheila left, Anya, Rebekkah, and I had a pleasant evening. Between rounds of Bananagrams, the girls took turns caring for Martin. I was glad for the chance put my feet up and not worry about the kitten. In fact, I was so relaxed that I fell asleep on the sofa and didn't hear Rebekkah leave. Either she or Anya kindly tucked a blanket around me and let me snooze.

The next morning my kid was in a great mood. I dropped her off at science camp. In short order, I arrived at the store. Dodie was already in her office and stuck her head out. "Can we talk?"

"Give me a sec, please." I put Gracie and Petunia in the doggy playpen and set Martin's cat carrier on my work table.

"What's up," I said, sliding into the chair across from her desk.

"I've been looking over our figures."

Uh-oh, I thought. Here it comes. She's going to fire me. We aren't doing enough for her to keep me on.

"I've decided to give Clancy more hours. Bama has other responsibilities, personal ones, that will take her away from the store."

My stomach twisted into a tight knot. I thought about finding an excuse to leave, to postpone the inevitable, but what good would it do? If Dodie was going to let me go, I'd better find out fast. That way I could start job hunting right away. But what sort of position would I find? All I knew was scrapbooking! The only other scrapbook store in the area was run by a woman who hated me. How would I take care of Anya?

I was in a real tizzy and missed what Dodie said next.

"Excuse me," I said with a shaking voice. "Could you repeat what you just said?"

"I want you to handle all our crops and special events."

"But what about Bama?"

"As I said, she has other responsibilities."

"But you could work around them."

"Yes, I could. However, she's great at doing bookwork and organizing our stock, so I think I'll have her stay focused on those areas. You have a real knack for teaching. People like learning from you. When Bama teaches them, they don't come back."

I'd noticed that. Bama had this way of making you feel stupid. She'd take projects out of your hands and fix them for you rather than guide you. In my humble opinion, the best teacher is the person who convinces you that you are capable. Not the person who makes you feel like a dope. That's easy to do, isn't it? To tear people down takes so little effort and thought. To build them up takes compassion, attentiveness, and sometimes ingenuity.

Dodie waited for my response.

I liked being in charge of crops.

Even with the recent disaster where Rebekkah hadn't done her share, I enjoyed thinking up great projects and watching them take shape under the hands of our customers. But beyond personal satisfaction, I needed money. Cold, hard cash. I'd learned the hard way to ask the next question. "What's in it for me?"

"I've given this a lot of thought. Talked it over with Rebekkah this morning before I came in. We think you should get a percentage of the profit from all the crops."

I nearly fell off my chair.

"That would be nice," I said, cautiously, "but until I know what the percentage is, I can't agree to the change in responsibilities. After all, this would mean that I need to put in more hours. I'm barely making above minimum wage right now."

"I realize that." Dodie named a hefty percentage. By my quick calculations, that could add a third more to my take-home pay. However, I'd learned a lot since coming to work at Time in a Bottle. Numero Uno: Jumping is for kangaroos. When given a new opportunity, take a deep breath and say, "I'll think it over." It's always smart to give yourself breathing room.

With that in mind, I hesitated. While I dithered, Dodie increased the offer by five percent.

Again, I said nothing.

This time she kept her mouth shut, too."

"Let me think about it," I said. "I appreciate your offer, and I'll get back to you."

CHAPTER 37

Tuesday evening...

Since I no longer have a husband to discuss matters with, I run all my important decisions by Gracie. She's a very, very good listener. When I rub those velvety uncropped ears of hers, she'll sit and listen for hours. I told her about Dodie's offer, and Gracie's expression spoke loud and clear: Do the math.

I hate math. I don't even like rulers.

Petunia had been listening in. He agreed. He didn't like rulers either. In fact, he wasn't keen on pencils. I knew this because I had to take one out of his mouth when I caught him chewing on it.

Properly assessing this new opportunity at the store would take a bit of homework. I looked over samples of past crop projects, and I scratched down numbers on pieces of paper. These notations helped me calculate the raw materials of each project and the amount we charged each attendee. If I could organize my scribbles properly, I should be able to calculate our profit on most of the projects I'd done. Because there'd been so many, there was a lot of figuring to do. And of course, those projects were now history. Even so, they'd give me a way to forecast the future. By the time that Sheila and Anya burst through the front door, carrying shopping bags filled with new school clothes, I had three sheets full of numbers, but still no handle on Dodie's offer.

A fashion show ensued. As always, Sheila had chosen stylish but appropriate clothes for my daughter. Anya looked cute as a button, a LaMode button to be exact. Thanks to my mother-in-law and her deep pockets, my daughter's fall wardrobe was pretty much complete. "All I need are things to goof around in," announced Anya as she rejoined us in the living room. "Tee shirts. Jeans. I need a new Cardinals tee to wear to school on team spirit days."

I had an idea where to get all those items at a hefty discount. I'd overheard Bama bragging to a customer about her ultra-cool wardrobe. Seems she shopped at Pedro's Planet, an upscale resale shop that catered to young consumers. Since teens often outgrow their clothes, Bama claimed that many of the selections had seen minimal wear. I certainly couldn't argue with the results. On that particular day, Bama wore an adorable black lace skirt over black leggings and a pair of chunky motorcycle boots. For a top, she'd added a thin knit sweater in a soft ballerina pink. From her ears dangled jet-black beaded earrings.

It was too edgy for me, but I had a hunch that Anya would love shopping at Pedro's. Fortunately, despite the fact that Sheila has given my child a taste for the finer things in life, Anya isn't snobbish. She's as excited about a cute secondhand blouse as one off the racks at Neiman Marcus. I made a mental note to get addresses and hours for the resale shop. Taking Anya there would make a nice surprise for my daughter, and it would definitely put points in my "cool mom" column.

"I can't thank you enough, Sheila," I said to my mother-in-law as I walked her to her Mercedes Benz.

"My pleasure. She's an absolute delight. You're doing a great job of raising her, Kiki."

Wow. Triple wow. Between Dodie's job offer and Sheila's compliment, I was flying high when I walked back into my house.

"What's this?" Anya stared at my scratchings on papers that littered our kitchen table.

I explained what I was trying to do.

"You need a spreadsheet."

"Probably, but I don't know how to make one."

"Geez, Mom, it's super easy," and with that my wonder child plopped down, opened an Excel file, and started a spreadsheet for me. In a few minutes, we were plugging in figures. In a half an hour, I had my answer. Yes, I would accept Dodie's offer, but I'd ask for an additional five percent. That would double my take-home pay. At the same time, I could assure her of an ongoing source of profitable events.

"Can you do this, Mom?" Anya turned her blue eyes on me once we'd generated our results. "I mean, don't you worry about running out of cool ideas?"

"Of course I do," I said. "But I intend to eat like a hummingbird and poop like an elephant."

"What?"

"A hummingbird takes in a lot of nutrients from a huge variety of sources. It eats all day long. But an elephant doesn't. So I intend to take in a lot of ideas from as many places as possible, and synthesize those ideas, and then I'll compress them into the best, coolest, newest projects ever."

Anya put her arms around me and rested her head on my shoulder. "I love you, Mom. You are something else."

CHAPTER 38

Wednesday late afternoon...

We kept digging deeper and deeper into the Marla Mess. Each peeled away layer brought to light a new level of disgust. The only way I could make it through the day was to remind myself of the pot of gold that sat at the end of this particular rainbow, the extra money. Having it put aside in savings would take away a lot of my stress. Since George died, I'd been living hand to mouth, worrying every day that I wouldn't be able to cover my bills, especially those once in a while occurrences that are part of life, like new tires for my car.

Although my back ached and my head throbbed, I could see we were making obvious progress. To keep myself from whining, I counted my blessings. This job had brought us Martin, extra cash, and a fresh desire to purge our house of any unnecessary junk. At the end of a day of hard physical labor, I had two new items for my gratitude list: I had a relatively cushy job, in that it didn't require brawn, and I could use my creativity in my work. Another add was my relationship with Rebekkah. It appeared to be back on course, and we seemed closer than ever. In fact, when she learned I'd be working at Marla's, she'd offered to take care of all the animals for me today. I wasted no time in saying yes. True to her word, she'd come by first thing in the morning and picked up my furry crew.

As I cuffed the sweat from my brow, I added their absence to my gratitude list. Today was beastly hot. Running home to let the dogs out and feed Martin would have meant climbing into a hot car. Rebekkah had saved me from further discomfort.

By the time Mert whistled us to a halt on Wednesday, I was staggering around. Even her scheduled water breaks weren't enough to keep me from dehydration.

"I can see you all are exhausted. Iff'n we keep at this, one of us will get hurt, sure as shootin', so I'm calling it quits for the day." Mert leaned against the trunk of the maple tree and savored what little shade it provided.

"Sis? Are we going to make Mrs. Timmons' deadline?" Johnny asked.

"If we keep hitting it hard like this, I'd say our chances are 50-50," she answered. "Now go on and git out of here."

After leaving Marla's place, the last thing I wanted to do was sit in the heat and the dust, watching a soccer game. But I wasn't about to let Anya down, so I raced home for a quick shower. As I rinsed off, I thanked my lucky stars that Jennifer Moore had offered to take the kids all the way out to the flats in Chesterfield, a suburb of St. Louis.

Even with her help, I'd be cutting it close to get to the fields before the game started. Because I was hustling along, I almost didn't pick up when Detweiler had phoned me as I was leaving the house.

"I hate to make this call," he said.

"Has Marla died?" I asked.

"Not that I know of."

"What's up? Did you find —" and I started to name my husband's killer, but Detweiler cut me off.

"It's Brenda. My wife." He nearly choked over that last word. "She heard that I dropped by your house. She's furious, and she told me that she has spies everywhere. I suspect she'll have people watching to see if we talk to each other at the soccer game." He paused. "You are coming aren't you?"

I gritted my teeth. There was no way I was going to give up attending my kid's soccer games just to make Brenda Detweiler happy. She'd shown up once at the store, and I'd been cordial, considering how rude she was. The second time she appeared at the door demanding to talk to me, Dodie sent her packing. I had no idea what was going on in the Detweiler marriage, but from an outsider's perspective, Brenda sure looked a lot like a whack job. I'd done everything I could to avoid her husband. Why was she so obsessed with me? I wanted to say to Detweiler, "Can't you control your own spouse?"

I, of all people, knew how silly that was.

I understood why he'd called. Anya couldn't be counted on to avoid Detweiler. She thought of him as a family friend. Therefore, he'd called because I needed to be warned so I could be pro-active.

How was I supposed to do that? Tell my kid to ignore Detweiler because his wife was jealous? Hot fury washed over me. I was not going to ask my child to change because Brenda Detweiler had a bug up her blouse.

In my silence, Detweiler continued. "I am very sorry, but Brenda doesn't understand."

"That makes two of us, bub." I pressed the "call ended" button.

I fumed the whole way to Chesterfield. I had pretend arguments with myself. But by the time I got there, I'd calmed down. "It is what it is," I mumbled, as I found a seat off by my lonesome at the end of a bleacher, feeling totally sorry for myself and hating the feel of grit on my skin. The soccer fields are nestled in a valley next to the levees of the Missouri River. In August, when everything is blooming, the pollen and the gritty dirt blow around in a circular pattern, restrained and contained in the bowl of the valley. When you sneeze, you realize how much dust you've breathed in.

I'm not a big soccer fan. Because I never know when to cheer, I try to follow what the other CALA parents do. If Jennifer's around, we sometimes sit together. Today, she had dropped off the girls and left. Unlike practices, soccer matches were well attended by parents, grandparents, and teachers from all over the St. Louis area. Minutes after my arrival, the bleachers were packed. School would be starting in a couple of weeks, and this gathering was an opportunity for a huge gossip-fest. Parents could swap tales about their children's teachers and commiserate about class schedules. I didn't join in. I had no desire to chat with the others. None at all. Thinking about Detweiler's call, I'd never felt so lonely at a game as I did now.

Detweiler stood at the other side of the field, his eyes scanning the kids restlessly, but I could tell he paid particular attention to Anya. Once as she was coming off the turf, she glanced his way and I saw him give her a thumbs up.

I wondered if anyone else noticed.

Even before Detweiler had called with his warning, I knew Brenda was keeping an eye on me. Once I found my mailbox filled with human excrement. Another time, all the air was let out of my tires. Recently my car was egged (what a waste—I was all out of eggs and would have gladly eaten them!), and my windows were soaped while I was in a local library teaching a class on journaling.

At first I chalked these incidents up to mischief by my husband's killer, but these pranks were more childish than menacing. As time went on, I grew more and more confident that Brenda was behind the misbehavior. Just thinking of her spies watching my every move made me sick. Or maybe it was the heat. The setting sun beat down on us. The seats were hot on the back of my legs. This time, thanks to Detweiler's last minute call, I forgot to bring a bottle of water.

Big mistake. I wiped sweat off my brow as Detweiler came in from his position out on the margins of the field.

During a break, I peeled myself off the hot metal stands and my legs buckled. I'd have gone down if I hadn't grabbed the bleachers.

In a flash Detweiler was at my side. He offered me his bottle of water and I took it.

"Did you work at the Lever house today?" One of his arms supported me.

"Yes."

"Thought so."

"Any progress on that cold case?" I asked between gulps.

"Not much. Although we do have a few good leads. All of the women disappeared within a radius of five miles around Ladue."

That shocked me. Ladue is the most exclusive suburb in St. Louis. The police presence there is above average, because wealthy citizens chip in to pay for extra security patrols.

"That's just weird." I handed him the empty bottle. "Thanks. Sorry I drank it all."

"No problem." He steadied me. "You okay?"

"Yup."

"Be extra careful when you are out and about. There's enough to discern a pattern. Worse luck, the disappearances are happening more frequently. Whoever this creep his, his needs are escalating."

"Got it." I returned to my seat on the bleachers. Despite how hot the metal was on the back of my bare legs, I shivered as I thought about what I'd learned.

CHAPTER 39

Anya wasn't the strongest girl on her team or the toughest. However, in a mad scramble I didn't understand, she scored the winning point for her team. When it happened, Detweiler raced to my side, grabbed me, and gave me a spontaneous hug.

The other parents were cheering, but a few of them glanced our way. I tried not to worry about it, but I did.

Detweiler set me down, turned toward the field where the team was congratulating Anya. He cupped his hands around his mouth and yelled, "Woohoo! Way to go, Anya!"

A grin split her face from ear to ear.

Detweiler was filling a hole in her heart and mine. I could feel happy about that. But I also couldn't stop it. Our lives were intertwined; I couldn't turn back the clock.

We walked toward the car, the three of us. A woman bumped me hard with her shoulder and hissed, "Slut." The impact caused me to stumble. Detweiler had been talking with Anya, and his hand shot out to steady me.

"Stepped on a rock," I said. "No biggie."

"This calls for Ted Drewes," Detweiler said.

Just that fast, I told Anya to get in the car. I even tossed her the keys so she could turn on the A/C.

"Are you sure?" I couldn't believe this was the same man who'd phoned to warn me about his wife spying on us.

He leaned close so only I could hear. "Got another call. She decided to drive to Chicago to visit an old friend."

"I'm not into sneaking around," I said with my eyes darting over to Anya. She was on her phone, oblivious to our conversation.

Detweiler shook his head. "I was wrong to call you. I need to man up and remind Brenda that I have a job to do. As long as your husband's killer is on the loose, you are a part of my job."

He paused to rub the back of his neck. "Like I told you before, you and I need to talk. My situation is complicated. It's not what it seems and—"

His phone rang. He waved a "one minute" finger at me, stepped away, and came back. "That was Stan. He's got new information. I asked him to meet us at Ted Drewes."

I bit my bottom lip. "I am not going to be a party to—"

"Too late," Detweiler said. "Thanks to your late husband and your cat hoarding pal, you already are."

Hadcho joined us at the frozen custard stand.

I had my customary Terramizzou, and Anya ordered a "Dottie," named for Mrs. Drewes, and a mix of chocolate, mint and macadamia nuts. The guys ordered a Strawberry Shortcake (Hadcho) and a Southern Delight of praline pieces and butterscotch (Detweiler). Leaning against our vehicles, we stood in the busy parking lot, under the street lights, and enjoyed our treats.

As soon as we finished and Anya was back in the car, Hadcho gestured to Detweiler and me. "We're going to need your kitchen table, Mrs. Lowenstein. I've mapped out our cold cases involving those missing women. There has to be a pattern, but it might take a woman's eyes to see it. It might have something to do with where all of them shop. Are you game?"

"You could be helping us save someone's life," Detweiler added.

Call me gullible. "Sure."

I led the way to my house, driving through dark city streets in my old and battered BMW convertible. Anya was thrilled to have scored the winning point and after being refreshed by the frozen custard, she chatted non-stop. Usually we referred to her participation in sports as "character building," because her teams lost so often. I couldn't blame her for making the most of her triumph.

Out of the blue, my daughter said, "I can't wait to tell Gracie that I scored the winning goal!" It was unusual for us not to have a dog in the car, and we both felt our four-legged friend's absence. Gracie had become my guardian, my sounding board, and my best friend. Obviously, Anya felt the same.

As I pulled into my driveway, I noticed Rebekkah had left the porch lights on. I made a mental note to thank her for being so thoughtful.

That impulse didn't last long because Gracie galloped up out of the darkness to greet me.

"What? You aren't supposed to be running around," I said as Petunia raced up beside Gracie. "Anya? Help me. Grab Petunia. I've got Gracie."

"Mom? What are they doing running around? You said Rebekkah was dogsitting. They could have gotten hit by cars or stolen."

"I know, I know."

"If they're outside, where's Martin?" Anya's voice was high and shrill.

"I don't know. There has to be an explanation. He's probably inside. Just hang onto Petunia while I unlock the house."

But Detweiler had already pulled up and parked on the street. Spotting him, Gracie jerked out of my hand and ran toward the detective. "What happened here?" Detweiler called out to me.

Hadcho pulled up and parked behind Detweiler.

"Beats me. Rebekkah offered to take care of the animals," I said as I fumbled with my keys. "She and I will have a talk tomorrow."

Detweiler took Gracie by the collar, and since she loves him best of all the humans on earth, she happily pranced alongside of him, looking very, very pleased with herself that she nabbed the tall guy. Hadcho trotted past them and reached the back door first to hold it open for Anya who was struggling under Petunia's squirming weight. The knob turned easily in his hand.

Hadcho's face was illuminated by the yellow bulb in the security light over my back steps. "Stop right there. If the door is open—"

"You can't walk in. Someone might have broken into the house," finished Anya.

"Good girl," said Detweiler.

"Unless of course, you are with two cops." Anya grinned under the security light.

"Even then. You all wait here. I'll check and clear the house," said Hadcho.

I stood there in my back yard and tried not to feel grumpy. "Thanks a lot, Rebekkah," I mumbled.

The temperature had dropped with the sun. I was tired and worn out and I wanted nothing more than my second hot shower of the day. Instead, I had to stand here and wait. The comforts of my home were tantalizingly within reach. Mosquitos began dive-bombing me. Anya slapped at one on her forearm. When Hadcho didn't come back right away, Detweiler handed Gracie over to me.

"Stay here." He disappeared inside my house.

"This is silly." Anya leaned against the side of our house, which was a converted garage on the grounds of Leighton Haversham's large Webster Groves estate. Really, Leighton'd done a wonderful job of remodeling the place. At the time, he planned to use "my" house as a writing studio, but after a few abortive attempts to write here, he decided to remodel a small space in his attic instead. "I know it seems foolish, but in that tiny space, my imagination supplies the scenery. Up there, I don't have distractions. I actually get more writing done."

I wondered how Leighton's book tour was going. I shivered and waited. Anya smacked at another mosquito.

"They smell my sweat," she said.

"Uh-huh," I agreed.

Detweiler stepped out the back door. "You both need to get back in your car. Drive to Sheila's house."

"Why?" I did not want to put up with my mother-in-law tonight.

"Trust me." His eyes told me not to ask anything more.

"But we can't leave without Martin," wailed Anya.

"Martin?" Detweiler looked confused.

"The kitten!" I could scarcely get the words out.

"Right, right, right. You go on. I'll find him."

I nodded, took Anya by her free hand, and started for the car.

Detweiler yelled to me, "Stan and I'll be by later, when we know more."

CHAPTER 40

Wednesday evening...

Sheila and Police Chief Robbie Holmes were on their way to see a foreign film over at the Frontenac theatre. I called her. She said they'd be back late. I asked if we could spend the night.

"Problem?"

"A small one. Enjoy your evening. We can talk when you get home."

Anya cried all the way to her grandmother's house, while I did my best not to join her. She was sure something awful had happened to Martin.

I was, too, but I pointed out to her, "You know if Gracie was loose, she wouldn't let anyone in our house, honey."

"What about Martin?"

"I don't know. I'm not sure where Rebekkah would have put the cat carrier. I mean, if she put it on the kitchen table, someone would have had to get past Gracie—and that's not likely. See?"

"Can you call her and ask?"

"Sure." But Rebekkah didn't answer her phone. That figured.

"I'll keep trying to get a hold of Rebekkah," I told my daughter.

Anya showered and went to bed in the room that Sheila had decorated especially for her. Both dogs were upset by her sobbing, so they piled on top of her and licked away her tears.

When I checked on her later, you could barely see the top of Anya's platinum blonde head. It was nestled between Gracie's black and white muzzle and Petunia's brown and black smashed in pug face. In the sliver of light from the hall, I also noticed that my child had one arm around each pooch.

I hoped I'd have better news for her when she woke up.

Detweiler showed up an hour and a half later. Hadcho was right behind him. After they parked their cars, I heard their doors slam almost in tandem.

I opened Sheila's front door with my heart in my mouth, prepared for the worst possible news. All sorts of scenarios raced through my mind. None of them pretty. I stood with one hand on the doorframe and thought to myself, "It's all my fault."

I loved Martin. True, I hadn't owned him for long, but he'd forged a new bond between Rebekkah and me. He'd brought happiness with him, even though he was a lot of work. I admired his spunk. Since I'd been feeding and mothering him, I felt a pang of grief much deeper than there should have been, considering how briefly I'd known him.

But if he was gone forever, I'd survive and so would Anya.

I took a deep breath, squared my shoulders and stepped aside to let the two detectives in.

CHAPTER 41

"Thank goodness." I reached inside the cardboard carrier while Detweiler held it open for me. I cuddled the tiny kitten as I made myself comfortable on one of Sheila's kitchen chairs. "Poor little Martin. Everyone ran off and left you, huh?"

"I think he'll forgive you." Detweiler chuckled as he pulled over his own chair. "Martin's carrier was sitting there, undisturbed in your bedroom. As for the dogs pulling a Houdini, I suspect that Rebekkah didn't get the latch hooked on Gracie's cage."

"Rebekkah does have a habit of being inattentive to details," I admitted.

"When that creep broke into the kitchen, your Great Dane must have pushed open the crate door." Hadcho sipped his coffee. The smell of the hazelnut brew lingered in the air, a warm and delightful aroma. Because Sheila loved good coffee, and Robbie was also a connoisseur, I knew exactly where they kept a package of ground beans from Kaldi's. I'd put on a pot as soon as I heard that Martin was all right. I knew both the cops would drink a cup or two.

"Maybe Rebekkah put Petunia inside the crate with Gracie. She probably thought it would calm Tunie down. That would mean both dogs burst out at the same time. Neither of them are barkers, so it's possible that the intruder didn't realize what waited for him or her," I said.

"Imagine his surprise. Suddenly he has this huge dog chasing him, with a smaller dog tagging along behind. I imagine that little pug feels pretty brave when he's with Gracie." Detweiler smiled at me, a look that put butterflies in my tummy. The sensation stirred me to action. I got to my feet to warm up Martin's formula.

"Thank goodness, Martin is all right." I tested the formula on the inside of my wrist.

Hadcho drained the last of his cup. "More?"

"Yes, help yourself," I said. I probably should have gotten up and poured it for him, but I was too worn out.

"Any idea who did it? And how he or she got into my house?"

"You said it yourself, Rebekkah probably wasn't careful enough when she locked up," said Detweiler. "There were no signs of forced entry. Maybe your intruder saw Rebekkah pull up and drive away. I checked and from a parking spot on the street, you wouldn't be able to see someone getting in and out of a car. Those stupid spirea bushes block the view. Someone watching wouldn't know that Rebekkah was unloading animals. Especially since Petunia and Gracie are both so quiet."

"How bad is the damage to my house?" Now that the animals were fine, I could take whatever came next.

"There's excrement smeared on two of your walls."

Not so bad. It could have been worse. "Whew."

"Whew is right," said Hadcho. "What a stink."

"Fortunately, I think your intruder was interrupted before he or she could do any major mischief," said Detweiler.

I said nothing. I wondered if this was his wife's work. I hated to ask because I saw no reason to make him feel bad.

Detweiler guessed exactly what I was thinking. "Brenda was out shopping with my sister. My mother told me as much."

"Who might have broken in?" Hadcho raised an eyebrow at me.

"How should I know?"

Hadcho shook his head and withdrew his notebook from the pocket of his navy blue jacket. "I took the liberty of calling your pal Mert and asking her to come clean your house tomorrow. You don't need to see that mess. Your renter's insurance should cover it, and seeing it'll just upset you. She told me that two members of Marla Lever's family threatened you yesterday. I'd like to hear about it from you. Not secondhand."

I told them about the visit from Allen Lever and Devon Timmons.

"Both men seem to blame me for calling the authorities."

"Could either of them have done this?" Detweiler asked.

"I don't know. Maybe. Maybe not. Someone also knocked into me tonight after the field hockey game and called me a 'slut.'"

"Is that what happened? You said you stumbled."

"I stumbled after I'd been pushed."

Detweiler closed his eyes. I could see the muscle along his jawline flickering. That happened when he got mad. "This has to stop."

"I don't think that the person at the game is the one broke into my house. CALA parents don't do stuff like that. It's beneath them. I mention what happened because, it could have been anyone, couldn't it?"

Hadcho smiled. "You seem to have a talent for getting in the middle of tough situations. But my money's on one of the yoyos who visited you at work yesterday. Mert Chambers thinks they're both a couple of idiots."

The front door opened and we heard voices. Sheila and Robbie Holmes were home.

CHAPTER 42

Since the two cops had downed enough coffee to keep Seattle sleepless all night, and I was still shook up over my pets, I needed a distraction. I suggested that we brainstorm the cold case file that Hadcho and Detweiler were tackling.

"No dice, young lady. You're a civilian," Robbie said right away. He and Sheila were old sweethearts from their high school days, and gradually I'd come to know the Chief of Police. A nice man. A bit stiff sometimes. Protective. And he melted whenever Sheila spoke to him.

"It's more important that we make sure that neither Allen Lever nor Devon Timmons was behind the vandalism tonight," Detweiler said. "We still don't know if anyone in Mrs. Lever's family was involved with the corpse we found at her house."

He turned to me and asked, "When is your landlord coming back to town?"

"Next week. Monday or Tuesday."

"Sweetie, can Kiki stay here until then?" Robbie asked Sheila.

"Of course she can. She and her menagerie." My mother-in-law, aka Ice Queen, positively glowed when Robbie talked to her, making the denim blue of her eyes more vivid in contrast to her snow white hair.

"Sorry about that," I said with a shrug.

"It's okay," said Sheila. "This little one isn't much trouble."

"Now that I'm taken care of, could I say something? I have an idea."

They turned to me expectantly.

"I know that the corpse at Marla's house piqued your interest because of the women who've gone missing here in St. Louis. It must be hard to find a common thread. Why not color code certain themes?" I explained how Anya's fourth grade teacher taught the kids to use a pink highlighter to code dates, a green highlighter for places, a blue highlighter for names, and so on.

"Would that help? Maybe a connection would jump out at you."

Robbie's glance toward Detweiler was anything but warm and fuzzy.

"I mentioned the case to Kiki, because I'm worried about her spending so much time at Marla Lever's house," Detweiler said. "Tonight proves that my concern was justified."

"I always tell my officers to trust their guts, Chad, so I suppose I've walked right into this one. That said, Kiki, you cannot share anything you've learned about that cold case. Not with anyone, understood?"

"I doubt that I know anything that hasn't been made public."

"There have to be common denominators," Detweiler said. "No serial killer could get away with grabbing these women unless he happened on a method that worked. That's simple logic."

Robbie stared at me and then at Detweiler for an uncomfortably long spell. Finally, he said, "Kiki, you're right. I am worried that the woman found on Mrs. Lever's property was the victim of our cold case perp. Chad has a point. You do need to be extra careful. That mess at your house might have been a warning from a murderer who's getting bolder with each kill. Whatever you do, don't go to the Lever home alone. Or back to your house without an escort."

"I won't," I said. Suddenly everything caught up with me. "If you'll excuse me, I've had it. I'm going to bed."

CHAPTER 43

Early Thursday morning...

I did a double-take at the sight of Robbie Holmes in an apron puttering around Sheila's kitchen. Fortunately, I keep a spare set of clothes at my mother-in-law's house. Otherwise I might have trooped downstairs wearing nothing but a tee shirt and panties. That would have been embarrassing for both the top cop and me.

"My meeting was at six and over quickly," he said, in a total non sequitur as the tips of his ears turned pink. "We've got a company installing a whole new wiring system at the police department. I figured I might as well work from here."

He must have felt weird, too, or he wouldn't have volunteered so much information. I had no doubt that he'd stayed overnight, but it wasn't any of my business. He and Sheila were both widowed; they were free to carry on as they wished.

"Were the colored pens helpful?" I asked to cover how awkward I felt.

He dodged my question. "Eggs? Waffles? Pancakes? Bacon? Sausage?"

I never turn down food. At my direction, he sautéed onions, mushrooms, red bell peppers, and a little diced ham. He added the veggie mix to Eggbeaters, topped it with a slice of 2% American cheese, and slid the finished product onto my plate. All the while he was wearing a lavender apron trimmed with ruffles and white lace.

I spread Brummel & Brown butter-flavored yogurt spread on a piece of sourdough Melba toast and crunched my way to heaven. Sipping a yummy mix of low-fat hot chocolate and coffee added to my joy. Is life good or what?

"Did my suggestion about the colored pens help at all?" With my tummy full, I felt brave enough to ask a second time.

"See for yourself." He took the chair opposite of me and then pushed a chart my way.

Quadruple wow. Robbie trusted me!

A rustling sound caught my attention. The noise came from the floor between us. I looked down to see the cat carrier.

"Martin!" I said with a jolt.

"Sheila already fed him. She was up early," and again he didn't meet my eyes. "I'd be happy to drop off Anya at the Science Center. It's on my way to the station. One of us can pick her up at the end of the day unless you have an objection."

"No, none at all. Thanks. That's very kind of you." Glancing at the charts, I could see that all of the women had three or four matching traits: kids, residences or workplaces within a ten-mile radius of downtown St. Louis, pet ownership, and body type. They were all very, very thin. I focused on their weight right away. Since I struggle constantly with being twenty pounds overweight, that probably said more about me than about the missing women.

"I've been meaning to talk with you about Sheila," Robbie said.

"Uh-huh." I was only half-listening.

"I know that the two of you haven't always gotten along," he said. "But I also know you've grown closer lately. I wanted to ask if you have any objection to us getting serious."

Considering that I was sitting in my mother-in-law's kitchen, eating her food, after spending the night under her roof, what could I say? It certainly wasn't up to me to decide what sort of relationship Sheila had with Robbie Holmes.

"Why would I have an objection?" I asked.

"Because I'm not Jewish."

"Neither am I."

"Really?"

"I agreed to raise Anya as a Jew, but I never converted."

"Ah." He seemed relieved. "Are you working at Marla

Lever's house again today?"

"Not today. Tomorrow. I have to go to the store today." I turned my attention back to the chart. "I suppose the part about being pet owners isn't surprising. Given that 63% of all American households have a pet. More specifically 34% own cats and 60% own dogs."

"How do you know that?"

"I did the research because I was offering a class on making pet albums."

"You're right," said Robbie. "There isn't much there to work with, but I'm thinking we can go back to their friends and family and see if within those categories there are more connections. Like if their kids all take gymnastics from the same place. Or they all used the same vet clinic. Whatever it is, we'll find it."

Robbie held out his hand, and I gave him back the chart.

"Don't worry your pretty head over this." Robbie tucked the papers into his briefcase. "Sooner or later, we'll find a common thread. Or the killer will get sloppy. How many bodies can you hide? And for how long? Unless this creep buried them in the rolling farmlands of Missouri, someone is bound to find a corpse somewhere."

"Like in a freezer?"

"I know you don't want to believe that Mrs. Lever killed her neighbor, but you're familiar with Occam's Razor, aren't you? The law of parsimony?"

"Given two competing theories, the simplest is most likely the correct one?"

"That's right." He tugged off the apron and reached for his tie. Without the benefit of a mirror, he wrapped the silk length around his collar and knotted it expertly. The whole action, smooth and habitual, reminded me that he'd been solving crimes for most of his adult life. As he moved past me, a whiff of lime-scented after-shave came my way. Robbie Holmes typified the term "avuncular." In his work he could be a real son-of-a-gun, but toward me he'd never been anything but kind.

"How did she get the woman into her freezer? It's not like Marla Lever was a body-builder."

"She rolled the body onto a blanket. She pulled the blanket along the floor and hoisted the body up to the freezer. Maybe she tied a rope around an overhead pipe and used leverage. How did the Egyptians build the pyramids?"

He had me there. "How did Mrs. Newcomber die?"

"Battered to death with a baseball bat. Probably chloroformed first. Maybe even tasered. We're still waiting on the autopsy. Stan Hadcho has gotten her credit card records. He's trying to piece together who saw her last and when that was. Unfortunately, it takes longer in real life than it does on TV."

"You think Marla Lever was strong enough to beat someone to death with a baseball bat?"

Robbie smiled at me. "You really don't know much about baseball, do you?"

CHAPTER 44

Thursday morning...

"Where's Trudy?" I asked as we gathered under Marla's maple tree a little later.

"Just get dressed, okay?" Mert handed me a Tyvek uniform.

She's usually upbeat, so I quietly suited up and didn't say anything else. Johnny joined us, putting on his Tyvek suit, and not saying a word either. Mert's son Roger joined us, but the expression on his face told me that he wasn't in a good mood either. I decided to keep my distance from the Crabby Chambers Clan.

At Mert's direction, I went upstairs to where Trudy had been working and started taking knickknacks off the crowded shelves in what had been Marla's bedroom. They'd already been photographed. My job was wrapping them carefully in unprinted newspaper and packing them into a sturdy box. For more than an hour, I worked steadily. Something niggled at me, told me that I wasn't paying attention. I chalked it up to the general tension in the air. Usually Mert alerted us when sixty minutes was up, but this morning I put in ninety minutes before she stopped me for our mandatory water break. Since her expression still forecast stormy weather, I held my tongue. I drank my water and returned to the second floor. After another ninety minutes of quiet, Mert popped her head into the bedroom. "How's it going?"

"Fine." I waved my arm to show her the progress I'd made. All of the shelves were clean, except for a foot and a half at one end.

Marla's cat figurines had been so numerous that she'd balanced them on top of each other. I'd managed to pack them up. Only one small pile remained.

"Sorry I was such a grump this morning."

I shrugged. Mert knew my house had been vandalized. Didn't

I deserve a little TLC? At the very least, she could have greeted me by asking how I was. Instead, she'd been nasty to me.

Sure the pay for this nasty work was grand, but I'd rather be putting in my hours at Time in a Bottle. Especially since Dodie and I had come to an agreement that would pay me handsomely for profitable special events. As I packed up the world's ugliest collection of china cats, my mind was free to roam. I'd thought up about a million totally cool ideas for scrapbook and papercrafting events. My fingers almost itched to get back to crafting.

"Come on, don't be mad at me," Mert said.

"I don't like being fussed at; I'm keeping my mouth shut."

"I deserve that. Sorry about what happened to your house. I'm worried that Devon or Allen decided to target you. On top of that, I don't think we'll get all this done by five. Especially since Trudy went AWOL."

"She's really missing?" I stopped what I was doing. "I don't understand."

"I don't either. I stopped by to pick her up this morning, and her mother said she went out last night and didn't come back."

"You are kidding."

"No, and since I ain't paid her yet, I'd have thought she would have gotten her skinny little butt in the pickup truck this morning bright and early."

"I need to make a phone call." I pushed my way past Mert.

"You leaving, too?"

"No," I said hurriedly. "I'll tell you later. Just trust me."

But she didn't. Not entirely. Coming right on my heels, Mert followed me down the stairs and out the front door where I could get phone reception.

Detweiler listened carefully as I explained about Trudy disappearing. "She has dark hair and she's super thin, like all the other women who vanished."

"Let me talk to Mert, please."

I handed her the phone. None of her responses to his questions encouraged me. She volunteered Trudy's last name, her address, and her phone number. There were a few other quick "yes" and "no" answers. When she finished and handed my cell phone back to me, the frown on her face had deepened.

"Do you really think...?" she paused.

"I don't know. Let's hope she had a hot date and spent the night. Maybe she lost track of time, and she'll call you any minute and ask for a ride."

"Somehow," Mert said, "I don't think that's going to happen."

CHAPTER 45

While I had been working upstairs, Roger had been mowing the grass. During a water break, Johnny told me that Roger had used a machete to hack down the overgrowth. "By the time he finished, he had a terrible sunburn and more chigger bites than I've ever seen."

"He owed me," grumped Mert. "I bought him a new pair of basketball shoes."

"I'm not saying he shouldn't have helped you. I'm just being sympathetic to my nephew. See, I've been working on my tender side," said Johnny with a wink at me.

"Where is Roger?" I asked.

"A friend came and picked him up when he was done. Since he does lawn care around the neighborhood, this wasn't such a big deal," said Mert in a grouchy voice. "It's not like I asked him to climb up the Sears Tower and wash the windows."

"Except that he'd never seen grass as thick as this," continued Johnny. "Or as strong and healthy, despite the fact we've had such a hot summer with so little rain."

"Who cares," Mert said and flounced off.

"She can snort and paw the ground all she wants," said Johnny, "but Roger and I have big plans. We want to own a landscaping business together. He's taking business classes. When I get done paying Sis back, I'm going to take horticultural classes at night."

"Really? Good for you. Did you get a chance to go over and see Mr. Ernest's place? Trudy had been pretty impressed with his plants." I poured cold water on an old bandana and wrapped it around my neck.

"While you were upstairs, I went over to return his recycling bin. At first, he didn't answer the doorbell. Then he opened his front door a crack. All I can tell you is he must have sunk a boatload of money into the plants over there. Got one of them miniature greenhouses, too. But he made it clear he wasn't interested in making my acquaintance."

When the break was over, Mert assigned me the job of wrapping up Anthony Lever's toys.

I would have rather shoveled dog and cat poop all day long, because touching that little guy's clothes and smelling his pungent sheets brought tears to my eyes. Any parent would recognize the smell of childish sweat. It's that iconic. Marla had not only kept Anthony's room as a shrine, she must have kept the door shut, because there was no evidence of cats. Only the funky scent of plastic toys, dust, and little boy.

His collection of trucks, cars, plastic tools, a miniature baseball bat, small Army action figures, and superheroes nearly put me over the edge. As I worked, my limbs grew heavier, as if I'd stepped into a blob of amber, and now it slowly congealed around me. Mingled with the natural sadness of this unnatural space was my fear that I'd never have another child. Silly as it sounds, I'd always wanted to have a little boy. Anya thrilled me. I adored my daughter, but I wanted to watch a boy child grow. Touching all these symbols of a boy's inner life set my internal clock to ticking.

At a quarter till five, a car door slammed. The noise caused me to look up from the box I was packing. A familiar voice lured me away from my work. I peered out the window. Detweiler was leaning against his unmarked Impala, waiting for Mert to come over and talk with him.

Their hands moved in animated gestures. Mert pointed to my window and motioned for me to come down. A glance at my cell phone told me it was quitting time.

"Cute lunchbox," said Detweiler as I joined him. Mert shook her head and walked away.

I held up the grinning Cheshire Cat that Anya had given me for Mother's Day. "Thanks. A good reminder to smile. Are you going to tell me what's happening with your cold case? With Trudy? Or am I a civilian again?"

"Let's go sit in the shade. I think Johnny should know what's happened, since he's the only man on your team."

Mert took her accustomed place under the maple tree. She didn't look up as we approached. To my shock, she flicked a tear from her face, which surprised me because she rarely ever cries.

"Trudy is unofficially officially missing," said Detweiler, after he shook hands with Johnny. They had a wary relationship. Johnny offered the cop a cornbread muffin, but Detweiler waved it away. I took two of them, because they were small.

"Mrs. Squires, Trudy's mother, is understandably upset. It's too early for her absence to be an official missing person case, but it doesn't look good. Especially after Trudy's cell phone was discovered in a parking lot outside a bar in Soulard."

Soulard, the old French section of St. Louis, was a happening place, especially for singles. The cobblestone streets and old storefronts gave the neighborhood a fantastic old-world feel. But it's location on the banks of the Mississippi also brought a shadowy feel to the area. I wouldn't want to walk around there after dark. Not alone.

"Couldn't she have taken off with a date?" asked Johnny. "Maybe she hasn't gotten home."

"Could be," said Detweiler. "But your sister pointed out that Friday's payday. Mrs. Squires says her daughter was looking forward to getting and cashing her check. At the very least, Trudy could have asked Mert for her money today if she didn't intend to stay on the job."

No one said anything for a long while. I helped myself to another piece of cornbread.

Detweiler continued, "My partner Stan Hadcho and I've been working on cold cases involving missing women. Trudy's disappearance fits the pattern. The abductor seems to prefer dark haired, thin women, ages thirty to fifty."

"That also describes Mrs. Newcomber," I said. "The corpse found in the freezer."

"Mr. Chambers," Detweiler said, "I'm asking you to be particularly observant. It looks like this guy has targeted dark-haired women, but I think any woman in that age range is at risk. Please keep an eye on Kiki and your sister."

"It don't really matter," said Mert, as she looked off in the distance. "This here'll be our last day. We're going to get fired. Ain't no way we can get this done tomorrow like Ali Timmons wants us to."

CHAPTER 46

I was hanging up my Tyvek suit in Marla's garage when Mert stopped me. "Toss that. Grab Trudy's off that there hook and toss hers, too. If we still have a job, you can get a new one tomorrow.

Ali Timmons text-messaged to say she wanted to talk with me."

"I wonder what about."

"Whatever it is, it cain't be good," said Mert. "Dag-nab that Trudy. I'm worried sick about her. If I wasn't so concerned, I'd be madder than a snake with a sunburned belly."

Very carefully I carried both Tyvek suits to the Dumpster. However, that cup runneth over, so I took both suits over to a box of black plastic garbage bags that Mert had opened. With my gloved hands, I wadded up my suit and shoved it into the void of a bag. I started to do the same with Trudy's, but I felt a small rigid rectangle of resistance. Carefully teasing the suit flat, I discovered Fred's business card. On the back was a handwritten phone number.

"You might want to see this." I showed the card to Detweiler.

"Trudy made a trip by herself to Fred Ernest's house day before yesterday to see if we could borrow one of his recycling bins. She was a real flirt. Trudy probably logged this number on the back into her iPhone. She'd just gotten that phone and was crazy about it."

"Stan's checking calls to and from her iPhone as we speak."

I'd no more than handed the card to him when a black Nissan Ultima pulled up and parked in front of Marla's house. Pamela Bertolli, the real estate agent I'd used when I sold my house, climbed out from behind the wheel. Catching sight of me, she waved and I waved back. Leaving Detweiler, I ran over to the car.

"Hey, Pamela. How are you?"

"Kiki, how lovely to see you." Pamela made a move to hug me, but I waved her away. "You don't want to touch me. I'm disgusting times two."

"Oh, dear." Pamela wore her hair swept to one side in the classic curves of the modern art museum in Bilbao, Spain. On anyone else, such a style would have seemed ridiculous, but Pamela pulled it off. Studying me, she said, "You're not involved in this mess, are you?"

I explained that I was part of the cleanup crew. "I bet you're here to help Mrs. Timmons determine whether she can put two houses on one lot?"

"No, sad to say, I'm here so Mrs. Timmons can sign paperwork to end our relationship. Unfortunately Mr. Timmons doesn't want to work with me. I've been told he's found a big name agent to deal with. However, he was happy enough to talk to me when he needed to know about what this lot might be worth."

I just bet he was, that little weasel. How like him to use Pamela's expertise early on, but then want to sign with a big name agent. Bait and switch, wasn't it?

"I'm sure all the nearby lots will go up in value once this place is knocked down. Mr. Ernest said as much."

"Oh, him." Pamela crossed her arms over her chest and looked away. "He could have never afforded his place if he hadn't inherited it. Knocking down Marla Lever's eyesore will enhance his home's value. He's done as much as he can to block the view of this place, adding expensive landscaping and shrubs." She patted her hair. "Are you still single, dear?"

"Yes."

"Steer clear of that one. Even though I've known him his whole life, he gives me the willies."

I bid Pamela goodbye and walked back to my car. Detweiler was waiting in his Impala to follow me to Sheila's house.

CHAPTER 47

Hadcho was there at Sheila's when Detweiler and I arrived separately. Robbie Holmes was exactly where I'd left him, but the kitchen was now clean. Linnea, my mother-in-law's maid, bustled around making dinner. She moved to hug me, but I explained that I was too gross to touch.

"I'd like a raincheck for that hug. Can I have it after my shower?"

"You've got it, sugar," said the black woman. "I'll make you a little snack to hold you until dinner, darlin'. You're probably plum worn out. Working in that heat. I never."

The effect of the temps, the emotion of Anthony's room, and the worry about Trudy piled up on me. While the men spread their paperwork on Sheila's dining room table, I hauled myself upstairs. Sheila kept all her guest bathrooms filled with luxurious soaps, shampoos, and skin softeners. For a long while, I stood under the showerhead, enjoying the feeling of water sluicing over my skin and knowing it carried away the stink of the day. When I climbed out, I wrapped myself in the thick terry robe hanging on the back of the bathroom door. I planned to get dressed, but exhaustion overtook me. As soon as my backside touched the bed, I quit fighting the urge to take a nap. I couldn't have been asleep very long when my phone rang. I recognized Mert's number and answered with a groggy, "Hello?"

"Roger and his pal cleaned the poop off your walls," said Mert, "but he thinks a new coat of paint is in order. You want them painted the same color? Roger can ask Mr. Haversham if he's got extra paint stashed somewhere. You got your landlord's cell phone number? Can you get in touch with him?"

"Actually, I'd like to change the color, and I know that Leighton won't mind."

"The walls will need to dry from all the scrubbing the boys

did," said Mert. "You've got time to think over what you'd like."

"How did your meeting with Ali Timmons go?"

"All right, I guess. She wasn't happy that we weren't all the way done, but she knew we'd been working hard."

"Are we working tomorrow?"

"Not until one. Ali's planning to get a man from a local gallery to come look at those totem poles we found. She got all excited thinking they might be worth good money. Between you and me, I wouldn't let one of them near my house with a ten-foot pole."

Mert obviously wasn't listening to herself or she would have caught the irony. To my credit, I didn't remark on it. Instead, I kept my mouth shut and listened as she prattled on.

"I told Ali Timmons how full the Dumpster was, and asked her what she wanted me to do with a couple of rugs her mother's cats had used as potty boxes. They looked to me like they might have been worth something once upon a time."

I nodded as I listened, even though she couldn't see me. But then I had a brainstorm. "Mert, where's the poop? I haven't seen any. How come Marla didn't have any potty boxes? Did you toss them out? Because I didn't."

"You worry about the strangest things," she said with a chuckle. A silence followed, as I listened to her breathing. "I didn't find any potty boxes. Not even on Day One. Johnny found three or four big bags of litter in the garage."

That wasn't surprising. Those of us accustomed to Midwestern winters often loaded our cars down with bags of cat litter when the seasons changed. When sprinkled on ice, the bits of grit gave our tires a better purchase on slick surfaces, while the weight gave our tires more traction.

"Marla had cat litter for her pets, but where were the boxes? No food bags either. Why would someone take those? It's remotely possible that Marla tossed her old cat litter trays to buy new ones because company was coming, but why would she dump her food bags, too? We know her son brought her litter, but there weren't any signs of it. Why? How could she have run out of all the food and all the litter and all the boxes at once? Right before my visit? That doesn't make sense."

Turning the pieces over in my mind, I half-dozed off. Garbage in, garbage out. But how and why? I thought about Martin. About feeding him and making him poop. The food went in, the food went out.

"Kiki?" Mert prompted me. "You still there?"

"Kiki?" Linnea's voice drifted up to me from outside my door.

"Honey? You ready for something to eat?"

"Got to go," I said to Mert. "Call you later."

CHAPTER 48

Detweiler had news for me when I joined the men at the dining room table. "That was Allen Lever's cell phone number on the back of Fred Ernest's card. You were right; Trudy Squires had added it to her phone directory."

"Does he have an alibi for last night? What happens next?"

"Can't answer that. Since Lever lives in Belleville we've got a problem," said Robbie. "We don't have jurisdiction in Illinois."

Linnea toddled over to give me that hug. "Your hair's still wet," she said, clucking over me. "Let me get you one of those headwraps Miss Sheila likes so much."

After she left the room, I asked, "Where is Sheila?"

"She should be back any time from picking up Anya. I'm here because they're working on the Internet at the police station."

"And because Linnea treats us like royalty," said Hadcho, eying a plate of oatmeal cookies the maid set down at his elbow.

"Go on with you." Linnea gave him a playful slap on the arm as she returned and handed me the turban. "Kiki, I made you a snack to hold you until your supper, honey. Freshly brewed iced tea, too."

Her iced tea is the best in the world, partially because she always adds fruit juices or mint to the mix. After downing one tall glass, I asked, "More please?"

"Bless your heart, of course." Linnea took my empty glass and set down a plate of turkey slices wrapped around string cheese.

"You look all beat up, honey." "That's it!" I slapped the table top. The three of the men stared at me.

"Did anyone outside of your department know that Mrs. Newcomber had been beaten with a baseball bat?"

"No," Robbie said. "Except for you."

"Day before yesterday, Fred Ernest wandered over to talk to us. He mentioned that Mrs. Newcomber had been beaten with a baseball bat. How would he know that? To top it off, Fred Ernest knew that Marla was having a scrapbook party at her house. I doubt that her kids did, seeing as how they were all mad at her. Maybe he's the one who tripped the circuit on Marla's A/C."

"Right, but why?" Hadcho asked.

"To set Marla up as a murderer," I said. "She couldn't defend herself if she was in a coma. My visit was as good a time as any to make Marla look guilty. Johnny told me that guys in prison bragged about setting other people up to take the fall all the time."

"That's one explanation for what happened," said Detweiler. "Following your logic, the perpetrator messes with the A/C, convinced that the heat would do Mrs. Lever in. Maybe he or she even meant to unplug the freezer but didn't get the chance. Your early arrival interrupted someone's plans."

"We're back to my original question, why?" asked Hadcho. "How does Fred Ernest benefit?"

"Her place was an eyesore and depressed the neighborhood property values. If he got rid of Marla, a new neighbor would move in."

All three men glanced at each other, and I realized that a message had passed among them.

"But we still don't know who killed Mrs. Newcomber or why," said Hadcho. "Unless Mrs. Lever actually did the deed herself and stuffed the woman in her freezer."

"What if the killer turned off Marla's air, let her swelter, and crossed their fingers hoping that after she died, Mrs. Newcomber's body would be discovered—and Marla would be blamed for her neighbor's death. A slam-dunk."

"A slam-dunk?" Robbie waggled an amused eyebrow at me.

"I don't know much about baseball, but I love basketball," I said. "If Clancy and I hadn't arrived an hour early for that crop, Marla would have died."

Robbie cleared his throat. "There is another explanation. Mrs. Lever had an unusual amount of Tofranil in her system. That probably caused her to have a stroke. Since she had a prescription for the drug, it's possible she had decided to commit suicide. Maybe out of guilt for what she did to Mrs. Newcomber."

I sat there, stunned. "Why kill herself when she knew we were coming?"

"She wanted her body to be found, and so she chose her time frame carefully," said Robbie. "It's possible that Mrs. Lever miscalculated the number of pills she needed to take. Or that she forgot you were coming early. Sorry, Kiki, but I've been over all this with her family. They feel that the stress of having company pushed Marla Lever right over the edge."

My stomach turned a flip. I got up and ran to the powder room.

CHAPTER 49

After rinsing out my mouth and splashing cold water on my face, I went back to the dining room table. Linnea, that paragon of kindness, had removed the turkey and replaced it with a selection of dry crackers. My iced tea was gone. In its place was a steaming mug of hot tea. The sugar bowl was within easy reach.

"Look," said Detweiler, spreading his big hands wide to appeal to me. "You can't blame yourself. The Levers are all feeling guilty, and you're an easy scapegoat." I nodded.

"Those threats toward you? We get stuff like that all the time," said Hadcho. "Accusations, too. But here's the deal. What if you hadn't called us? Someone else would have walked into that house, sometime or another. We would have been involved. It's a matter of timing, that's all."

"I didn't tell you about their accusations earlier because I didn't want you to feel bad," said Robbie. "I'm telling you now because you need to stay vigilant. There's already been one round of vandalism at your house. Luckily you weren't there. You need to stay here under Sheila's roof until Leighton comes back. Then we'll see what sort of security devices we might add to whatever it is that you've got."

"Can you check out Fred Ernest?" I asked. "You have to admit, he's pretty creepy. And he did share Allen Timmons' number with Trudy. You could bring him in for questioning, because he lives on this side of the river."

Again, the men glanced at each other. They waited for Robbie to decide how much to tell me.

"We're doing our best," he said. "Other than hearsay from you that he knew Mrs. Newcomber was bludgeoned to death, we have nothing to go on. Forensics is examining her body. It's not like on TV where it's done instantly. So far they haven't found anything. Even if they do, we'd need a way to get DNA samples from Mr. Ernest for comparison. Right now we don't have probable cause. It's too early for me to ask the man to come down to the station and give us samples."

"But he gave Allen Timmons' phone number to Trudy and she's missing."

"He could have done that for all sorts of reasons. We can't draw a straight line from him sharing the phone number to her disappearance."

Sheila and Anya's voices burst through the back entrance. My child came running into the dining room and threw her arms around my neck. "Hi, Mom. Guess what? Gran and I went shopping for Martin!"

Sheila struggled under the burden of several plastic bags. Hadcho was closest to her, so he rose and helped her with the parcels.

"Cat litter pan, litter, scoop, catnip, toys, a cat collar, food, and dishes." Sheila looked pleased with herself.

"Isn't Martin's collar neat?" asked Anya, reaching into a bag and holding up a blue plaid strip of fabric. "Look, Linnea! It's got this elastic piece so if he gets it caught, he won't choke."

"Sheila, this is too kind of you," I said.

"Your hobby is scrapbooking, mine is shopping." Sheila flicked a strand of silver-white hair off her forehead. "Anya? Please set up the litter pan, like I told you. We can introduce Martin to the cat litter once you get it set up."

Hadcho carried the parcels up the stairs while Anya used a pair of scissors to cut open a big bag of Tidy Cat. Linnea cleaned a plastic butter tub for my daughter to use as a scoop. In short order, the litter pan was lined with newspaper and had a thick layer of clay particles inside. Anya surveyed her work with pride. After Hadcho returned, my daughter carried the pan upstairs, while Sheila carried Martin in his cat carrier.

My mother-in-law reappeared wearing a smile on her face.

"Everything is set up in Anya's bathroom. That little rascal knew exactly what that litter was for. I showed Anya how to clean up after him. She's giving him his bottle."

"That reminds me of another anomaly," I said to the cops. "Remember how Sherlock Holmes once solved a mystery because a dog didn't bark? Something is missing here. Several things in fact. Specifically, there are no cat food containers and kitty litter pans."

"That doesn't make sense. Marla marked on her calendar that someone with the first initial 'A' was bringing over food for her cats." Detweiler tapped a finger to a page in his notebook.

"That's right," I said. "No name, just an initial. But that doesn't make sense either because when we got there, we didn't find one empty bag. Not one. Nor any cans of cat food. Or any litter pans."

"Maybe she gave up on putting out litter pans. It sure smelled like she had." Hadcho chuckled.

"Come on. Despite all the crud we cleaned up, there must have been litter pans at one point. Marla mentioned it in her journal, and her son, Allen, told us that on occasion, he brought bags of it to his mother. Otherwise, there would have been even more of a mess on the floors. Allen also said he brought food, but I didn't see any bags or cans of it. Mert came up with a crazy idea that the bags of meat we found in the freezer were venison. Even so, that would have taken a lot of dead deer."

"Who supplied the meat?" mused Robbie. "Maybe there's another person involved in this. Someone else who had access to the house. A regular visitor."

"But someone who'd be so tidy as to toss out the cat litter pans? And the food bags?" wondered Hadcho. "Right before Marla Lever was due to have company? Did you find any signs of either in the trash bins, Kiki?"

I thought about his question. I clicked open my cell phone

and called Mert. I relayed the question to her and put her on speaker phone.

She took a minute to respond. "No. Huh-uh. And we brought all the trash bins with us. Every bin that's there is one that I brought. No garbage bags either. Why?"

"Nothing," I said. "Just curious. Talk to you later."

"Okay," Robbie said. "So this mysterious person turns off Marla's A/C unit, stuffs a corpse in her freezer, and takes out the trash. Including all signs of cat food and the litter pans. Why?"

"Don't forget, our mystery guest also dosed Marla with extra Tofranil," I said. "I'm still not convinced that she tried to kill herself. I talked to her the day before to remind her that we were coming, and she was excited. She definitely did not sound suicidal. I told her that Clancy and I would help her get ready. At that point, she could have told me to cancel. She was intimidated by Rebekkah but not by me."

"There's only one reason to get rid of the trash, the food, and the litter pans," said Detweiler. "There was something incriminating about them. But what?"

CHAPTER 50

"Is it possible that someone is poaching deer?" I asked. "We found a meat hook in the back of the garage. There were dried up deer hooves there and blood stains. Since season doesn't start until September, maybe one of the Lever-Timmons crew jumped the gun? If that's the case, the hunter could have been supplying Marla with deer meat all along."

"You're suggesting that this person panicked?" Hadcho asked.

"I'm thinking that he or she, but most likely he, supplied Marla with ground deer meat all year long—even out of season, which is illegal. Given the number of deer in the metro-St. Louis area, no one would have noticed them missing."

"But it would have still been against the law," said Robbie.

"We might have interrupted the person when he was cleaning out Marla's refrigerator freezer."

Detweiler frowned. "You think that this person gathered up all the food dishes and litter pans so there wouldn't be any forensic evidence of what the cats were being fed, short of examining the animals themselves."

"That would explain why Mrs. Newcomber was the victim. Maybe she figured out what they were doing. Remember, she did eventually get her cat back. What if she realized he'd been eating deer meat?"

"How would she know that?" Hadcho asked.

"If her cat had parasites, and her vet noticed them…" I got up and went into the next room where Sheila's laptop was running.

"Yup. Look here," I said as the guys came over to join me. "See? There are a variety of internal parasites that are deer specific."

A few more clicks took me to a zoological site that listed bacteria, viruses, and worms that could be transmitted from wild animals to domestic ones. For some there was no proof of transmission, just a high probability.

"Mrs. Newcomber retrieves her cat. The cat gets sick. Mrs. Newcomber takes the animal to her vet. The vet diagnoses the illness as a result of eating deer meat," said Hadcho.

"Now Mrs. Newcomber is really angry with Mrs. Lever. She shows up on the woman's doorstep. They fight. Mrs. Lever wins the fight—" Detweiler continued.

"With a little help from a baseball bat," I added.

"Mr. Ernest might have heard the commotion. He shows up in time to see what Mrs. Lever has done," said Robbie.

"She reminds him that he's the one who gave her the deer meat," Detweiler said. "Therefore, he's also to blame. He helps Mrs. Lever hoist Mrs. Newcomber's body into the freezer. While they're working together, she lets it slip that she's having a scrapbook party at her house."

"He's fed up with her messy place, and now he has reason to worry that she'll tell one of her new friends what she's storing in her freezer." I turned away from the computer and faced the guys.

"He can't let that happen," Detweiler said. "He knows she's taking Tofranil."

"Because when her car was on the blink, he took her around to do her errands," I said. "That's when he noticed her prescription."

"He gives her an extra dose of her meds." Robbie squinted as he thought this through. "Our creep helps her to bed, but before he vacates the property he flips the switch in her fuse box and turns off her A/C. With all the reports of people dropping like flies, he figures she'll drift quietly away. When her body is discovered, there'll be nothing to link him and the frozen corpse-sicle in her freezer. He'll be off the hook for hunting deer out of season, and he's done the neighborhood a service by making it possible for Mrs. Lever's dump to be replaced with a

McMansion or two. In fact, he probably sees himself as an all-around humanitarian. He takes care of the local deer population problem, feeds cats that would otherwise have starved to death, and when it all gets to be too much for him, he cleans up the problem by letting the world see Marla Lever's ugly mess."

I turned back to study the computer monitor. "There's a way to see whether we're wrong or not. I found bags of frozen meat in Marla's freezer. Mert took them home and put them in her trash. Stuff in the Dumpster won't get dumped until we're done, and she didn't want the mess to draw more flies. But her trash pickup isn't until tomorrow. If you want, I can call her and see if she'll snag a bag for you. It'll probably stink to high heavens."

I dialed her number. Robbie checked with Mert to make sure the trash hadn't gone out. Then he sent a squad car to pick up a bag of the ground meat. "Be sure to take a Styrofoam cooler and some Vicks. Ms. Chambers says that mess already smells terrible."

"Dinner is ready," said Linnea in a formal voice. "Miss Sheila expects all of you to get washed up and join her in the dining room. She's serving my special meatloaf. I made it just for all you gentlemen."

CHAPTER 51

Meatloaf would have been my last choice if you'd handed me a menu. Dead last. In fact, I would rather have gone hungry. A glance at Robbie, Hadcho, and Detweiler confirmed a similar reaction.

The men made lame attempts at dodging the invitation, but in the end, we all sat down at Sheila's beautifully appointed table. My daughter said grace. Linnea proudly served us…meatloaf.

Despite how good the dish smelled, I couldn't help but compare it with the bags of venison we'd been discussing earlier. My mind played a slideshow, starring pictures of protozoa and parasites. Ugh, ugh, and double ugh. Fortunately, when the platter came my way, I was able to take a pass by saying, "I'm watching my weight."

Under her breath, Sheila muttered, "About time."

The guys, however, couldn't get out of eating the main dish so easily. Detweiler once confided in me that typically he managed to push aside any ugly thoughts gathered in the course of a day's business. However, tonight, that strategy didn't work. The Internet search I'd conducted was too fresh in all of our minds. I watched curiously as each of the guys found a different way to cope with the problem: Robbie slathered his thick slice of meatloaf in ketchup. Detweiler gulped his quickly. Hadcho scooted his around his plate.

Meanwhile, I filled up on salad, veggies, and dessert.

By the time I'd savored the last morsel of Linnea's awesome strawberry shortcake, my eyes were so heavy that I could barely keep them open. I don't remember how I excused myself, but I must have, because I slept face-down on the duvet cover on the bed in the guest bedroom.

I awoke with a start, checked my face in the mirror over the dresser, confirmed the presence of railroad track seams running from north to south, and groaned out loud, thinking of my responsibilities. But there was no help for it. I needed to go downstairs and check that Gracie and Martin had gotten their food. The wonderfully comfy bed called my name, but I exercised maximum self-discipline and walked past it to the bedroom door. The sounds of adult voices drifting up from the first floor assured me that other grown-ups were awake. Surely Robbie or Sheila would know if my pets had been fed.

By the time I set foot on the last riser, I had to use the bathroom. Rounding the corner, I headed for the powder room off of Sheila's kitchen. Since I was in a hurry, I slammed right into Detweiler.

"Sorry," I mumbled as I tried to back away. The chance meeting discombobulated me. Being half-awake didn't help.

He grabbed my shoulders to steady me. "Hey, you just wake up?" His voice was low and husky.

I brought my eyes up slowly to his. "I fell asleep, but then I realized that Gracie and Martin—"

"They've been fed. Anya and Sheila took care of them. Robbie, Stan, and I have been going over the witness statements."

He didn't remove his hands from my shoulders. The warmth of them spread in a tingling rush, as if a million volts of static electricity powered through them.

"I'm glad you're staying here." His breath tickled my face.

"Why?"

"I'm worried," he said, in a near whisper. "The thought of you disappearing…"

"Like poor Trudy." I turned my face up to his.

"Right." He lowered his face ever so slightly and used the back of his hand to brush a clump of my curls away. His green eyes searched mine. "If anything happened to you…"

"You'd care?" I leaned in, closer, until our bodies touched.

"Of course I would." His hands slid down my arms, moving to encircle my waist. I watched as he swallowed, rapidly, and I felt his body responding to mine. How long had I gone without affection? Without touching or being touched? Numbing myself physically because I didn't want to experience the longing, this longing, this yearning to be closer than close?

He brushed his lips against mine. I stood on my tiptoes and answered his kiss with a deeper, hungrier kiss of my own, wishing that I could draw him in —

"Ahem." Sheila had come up behind us.

Detweiler and I jumped apart. Over Sheila's shoulder, I could see Anya's eyes, big and round and blue, staring at me.

What have I done?

CHAPTER 52

While Anya stared at me, Detweiler pivoted on his heel and took off down the narrow hall that led past Sheila's laundry room. He was headed for the back door. I wished I could follow along behind, but Anya blocked my way.

Nice. He'd left me to face the music, my mother-in-law, and my kid.

"Did you feed Gracie and Martin?" I had managed in a bit of a squeak.

"Yes." Anya's gaze was level and cold.

"Good. Did he, uh, do —"

"We took care of everything, Mom. Everything," said Anya.

"Anya has been incredibly responsible," said Sheila. The underlying unsaid message was: You haven't.

"I'm going back to bed." I was too tired, too woozy, and too confused to deal with this.

"Sweet dreams." My daughter's voice dripped with sarcasm as I climbed the stairs.

I crawled under the covers. Sleep came in fits and starts. I'd doze, wake up, touch my mouth, and wonder, "Did I dream that?" Then I'd remember Sheila's startled expression, and the angry look my daughter had worn as she stepped around her grandmother so she could see me better. Even though we'd sprung apart, the guilty expressions on our faces confirmed Detweiler and I had been doing *something.* With that unerring sixth sense kids have, Anya knew whatever it was had been rated M for Mature Audiences.

My face burned with embarrassment. I chugged all the water in the bedside carafe, but my mouth was still dry.

What have I done? I kept asking myself the same question over and over.

Moving restlessly in Sheila's guest bed, I threw back the

covers and stared at my waist. He had wrapped his arms around my middle. He'd told me that he cared. I mattered to him. He worried about me.

At least twice during the night, I got up and paced the guest room. By the time that the sun came up, brightening all the hidden corners of the room, I felt like I'd run a marathon. (That's never going to happen, but I can imagine it.) I didn't want to climb back into bed and surrender to sleep, to a place where I couldn't control my thoughts. Instead, even though it was early, I decided to get ready for work.

My mother-in-law, the Martha Stewart devotee, had thoughtfully cleared two dresser drawers for me and a space in this particular closet. Linnea, who thought Martha was a make-work joke, had washed and folded clothes I'd left behind. Rummaging through the neatly stacked items, I found an outfit I could wear to the store. I also found something suitable to wear to Marla's, if need be. I wondered what Mert would learn after she talked to Ali Timmons. Ali seemed like the sort of person who would withhold Mert's money as retribution if the police showed too much interest in her husband or brother. I hoped Mert had been paid up front.

I sighed. Mert was a good businesswoman. She'd probably gotten half up front.

I hoped so.

I didn't expect to see Sheila in the kitchen. I had figured that the noises down here had come from Robbie. But no such luck. I rounded the bottom of the stairs and saw her back, rigid as always, despite the fact she was wearing a bathrobe.

"Morning, Sheila."

"Morning." She started the coffee maker and depressed the lever on her toaster, but she didn't turn to face me. "Is there something I can make for you?"

This was good manners talking. She can't cook a lick. At least, not as far as I know.

"Thanks. I'll take care of myself. By the way, if I haven't thanked you for your hospitality, please forgive me. You've been wonderful."

"It helps to have Robbie around, doesn't it? He's usually in such a good mood." She shoved one hand into the pocket of her robe. A waft of her expensive perfume came my way. As usual, she smelled terrific.

"He's always been incredibly nice to me, and to Anya, of course."

The conversation sputtered to a halt. I suspected that she was waiting for me to say more, but I clamped my lips together in anticipation of spilling the beans. Their relationship was their business, not mine.

"Have you given any thought to getting married again?" Sheila poured herself a cup of coffee.

The question came out of the blue. Momentarily, I floundered for an answer.

"Not really."

"You're very young to stay single."

"You are, too."

"I guess. Robbie and I have been friends for decades."

"He's a good man."

"Yes, he is. I can't imagine being the wife of a law enforcement officer. I'm not sure that our relationship will go any further."

I didn't know what to say, so I kept my mouth shut.

"That brings me to the point I want to make." Still she didn't face me. I knew something was coming. I steeled myself for it. I didn't help her though. I didn't say a word. I simply waited.

"Chad Detweiler is obviously quite taken with you."

"That was a surprise to me, too. I mean, sort of. Caught me off guard. Did Anya say something?"

"As a matter of fact she did. She asked me if it was wrong for a married man to be kissing a woman other than his wife."

A punch to the gut. Her words hit me and hurt me and left me gasping for air. Even as I struggled, Sheila stayed as she was, refusing to face me.

"What did you tell her?" My voice came out in a squeak.

"I told her that it wasn't a good idea, but I went on to say that a mutual attraction can be very hard to resist." Quietly, she stirred her coffee.

"Oh."

"Especially when the two people like and respect each other, as you two obviously do." She added a bit more skim milk to her cup. I noticed her hand was shaking slightly. Standing here behind her, it was easy to see how it trembled.

"Anya asked me if a kiss was adultery, and I said that it wasn't, but again, it wasn't a step in the right direction."

"Thank you." I meant it sincerely. Sheila could have thrown me under the bus. I deserved it, kind of.

As I watched, she slowly rotated to face me. Her eyes had turned the color of frozen blueberries.

"I didn't do it for you. I did it for Anya." Sheila's tone sliced through all the baloney. "Don't make me regret it."

CHAPTER 53

"You look like twenty miles of bad road, Sunshine. Rough night?" Dodie greeted me as I walked into the storeroom.

Great, I thought, just what the world needs. Another amateur stand-up comedian.

"You could say that." I put Gracie and Petunia in the playpen. Martin had graduated to a large box where he could play and roll around. I set it on the floor near the dogs and grabbed their water dish to wash and refill it.

"Ready for another fun Friday night crop?"

The dog's water dish fell right out of my hands. With everything that had been happening at Marla's house, and in my personal life, I'd totally lost track of the days. Fortunately, my back was to Dodie. Otherwise, she'd have seen the look of pure panic on my face. To cover while I did a mental tap dance, I turned on the spigot and filled Gracie's bowl. Great. I had, what? Four hours to think of a project? And to come up with supplies?

"Absolutely," I said.

"Good, because we've got twenty people signed up."

Twenty? I thought about running screaming out of the building. What on earth was I going to do?

"What's happening with the food?" If she had that covered, I could cope with the make-and-take. Otherwise, I was toast. Burnt toast.

"My daughter told me she has it covered." Dodie looked pleased that she could point with pride to Rebekkah's efforts.

I resisted the urge to say, "Great, and I'm going to be featured in *Vanity Fair* this month with their list of the world's best-dressed trendsetters."

"Cool."

It wasn't cool. It wasn't great. It was a crisis. And I had to deal with it.

The good news was that racing around, trying to come up with a last minute project, took every bit of my concentration.

I should have been thinking about what to say to my daughter, how to apologize for my lapse in judgment, and how to avoid Detective Chad Detweiler. But I didn't have the opportunity to dwell on those weighty sentiments. I had to come up with a make-and-take project. Something thrifty. Something ultra-cool. Something we had the supplies for. Something that I could manage fast. I didn't have the time to cut out dozens of small pieces or round up supplies.

In my panic, I moved from supply cabinet to boxes to display racks and back to my worktable. As I moved, the pressure inside me built to a crescendo. I can't explain what happened next, except to say that the pressure got to me. Suddenly, I felt my throat tighten and tears popped out like I'd sprung a leak. I put my head down on the worktable and sobbed. Luckily for me, Dodie was watching one of her news shows on television. She didn't even hear the racket I was making.

I went through about a million, zillion tissues, pulling them one right after another out of the box. "Detweiler," I groaned. It just wasn't fair! I loved him. I couldn't help myself. He was the right guy for me. I'd known it for a long, long time. And he adored my kid. But he was off-limits. Totally out of the picture.

I could not risk my daughter's approval by keeping him in my life. Because, just as sure as I knew my name, if he was around, I'd be tempted. Lord knows, I'm not much for temptation. I'd rather just give in quickly and take the consequences than to hold off and suffer.

"It's not fair," I whined as I mopped my eyes. The lack of sleep and the overwhelming sense of loss culminated in one last burst of tears before I started hiccupping. I yanked the very last tissue out of the box.

The box.

I stared at it.

Dodie always bought those small vanity-size boxes of tissues. They took up less of a footprint than the regular, rectangular shapes. In our recycling bin, we must have had thirty empty boxes.

We would flattened them out and let them pile up.

I turned the tissue box over and over in my hands. Re-imagined, it would make a wonderful small album. The oval aperture would be a perfect frame for an album title or photo. The size was big enough for standard photos. The weight of the cardstock would make it easy to manipulate.

"You need a Diet Dr Pepper?" asked Dodie.

"You read my mind," I said.

"Whatever it is that's bothering you, Sunshine, you'll feel better about it when you've gotten more rest. Things always look their worst when you're tired." She scooted a cold aluminum can my way.

"Sheila called you."

"Yes, she did." My boss didn't even have the good grace to look embarrassed.

"That's not fair!"

"She was worried about you."

"I bet."

"She had good reason. You ran over her neighbor's mailbox this morning," said Dodie. "And you kept on going."

That shut me up. But not for long.

"I wondered what that bumpity-bump-bump-bump noise was."

"That was the sound of a once sturdy four-by-four being dragged down a city street."

"Argh," I groaned and rested my forehead on my arms again. "That'll be an expensive fix."

"Not really. Robbie and the neighbor discussed the damage. Seems that the neighbor had been wanting to put up a brick mailbox stand for years. Robbie offered to help. You're in the clear, Sunshine."

I groaned again. "Dodie, do you think there's only one person in the world for each of us? A soul mate? Just one?"

She fiddled with her Coke can. "That's what I tell Horace. That he's my one and only."

"Then you do believe it."

"No, but I'm a good liar. Especially when it counts. There's no reason for Horace to think he's replaceable. He's not. And I'm not about to go looking. But do I really believe we each have one soulmate? No. There are millions upon millions of people in this world. I think you could love and live with at least a handful."

I wiped my eyes and took a big drink of my Dr Pepper. "A handful. That many?"

"At least. Now get to work. I'm not paying you to sit around and wax philosophical."

She'd almost made it back to the stock room when I called out, "Dodie? Thank you."

"It's okay, Sunshine. My therapist's license never came through. The advice I gave you is worth exactly what you paid for it."

My cell phone chimed to tell me I had to change out of my nice top into the tee shirt I'd brought for another afternoon at Marla's Messy Mansion. I'd no more than turned the ringer off than the front door flew open and in walked Mert. Her hair was wet and slicked back into a ponytail, but she was nicely dressed in her usual "show off the merchandise" low-cut top and tight cropped pants.

"Uh-oh," I said to myself. This couldn't be good news. If she wasn't working, that meant that Ali Timmons had fired us. Slowly, I rose from the stool where I'd been sitting, collating, and stapling project sheets for tonight's make-and-take.

But before I could hail my friend, the door opened behind her and in walked Robbie Holmes.

Now I was really, really curious. Had he come to tell me I owed him for the busted mailbox?

"Good news," he said.

Mert didn't slow her pace. She pulled up the stool opposite of mine. I couldn't tell by her face what she was thinking, so I asked her, "Do you agree that it's good news? Whatever it is?"

"Sort of." She shrugged.

"We found Trudy Squires." Robbie continued, "She's alive. Scared. Shook up, but alive."

"You can say that again," muttered Mert.

"Where was she?"

"In a house of horrors," said Mert. "Fred Ernest had her tied up in his basement. He was waiting for us to finish at Marla's before he…"

Mert and Robbie exchanged long glances. He rubbed his neck.

"Kiki? You can't breathe a word of this. Let's go someplace private."

210 Joanna Campbell Slan

I ran back to tell Dodie that I was stepping out for a minute. Then I accompanied Robbie and Mert, climbing into his big police cruiser. He turned on the engine and cranked up the A/C. When we were settled, he said, "You were right and wrong about the meat in those bags."

"It weren't no deer. It was ground up people," said Mert.

I gagged.

"The missing women," clarified Robbie.

"How on earth?" I couldn't believe what I was hearing.

"That creepy Fred Ernest was helping Marla Lever, all right," said Mert. "He used her cats as bait. See, he'd take one with him in his car when he went looking for women to prey on. Then he'd let the cat out and tell the woman it was a stray and he needed help capturing it."

"That's how he lured the women into his car," I said. "And that's why they didn't fight him or take their purses along with."

"Exactly," said Robbie. "Once they got close enough, he'd chloroform them. The only question is how long did he use this method? I understood that her hoarding cats was a recent development, right?"

"Right," I answered, "but I've seen her calendars going ten years back. She's owned cats for a decade."

"Got it," said Robbie.

That's when it hit me. "So that hoist in the garage, where we thought one of the Levers was field-dressing deer…"

"Correct," said Robbie. "As you know, we sent a bag of what we thought was venison to the lab last night. This morning, when we learned it was human, Mert reminded us about the hook. Originally, of course, we used luminol in the garage and got a hit, but we thought the blood was from animals. So we sent the techs back in to check it out."

"It gets worse," said Mert. "You remember that woodchipper? That NorthStar brush chipper we found in the garage? It can take anything up to six inches wide. That monster was feeding his victims through that machine. Then he'd give most of the ground meat to Marla to feed to her kitties."

"That's why we couldn't find bags of cat food!" I shook my head in wonder.

"All the missing women were all thin, because he needed to shove their limbs into the chipper," said Mert. "That also explains why his lawn was so gorgeous. He'd drag that wood chipper over to his house, haul it into his backyard, and because he'd blocked all the sightlines, no one knew what he was feeding into the hopper."

"How did you find Trudy? Why did Fred give Trudy the phone number for Allen Lever?"

"Because they were working together," said Robbie. "Alfred Ernest and Allen Lever. A homicidal duo. It's not that uncommon. In fact, Fred groomed Allen to be his little helper. Oh, my gosh."

Robbie and Mert explained the rest, but I quit listening about halfway through as I fixated on the perils of being a single mom. Marla Lever had trusted her kindly neighbor, Fred Ernest, to be a good role model for her son. After losing her other son, Marla must have fretted over Allen, possibly even ignoring any of his faults. Under Fred Ernest's tutelage, Allen had exploited his mother's weaknesses for years.

"Allen or Fred Ernest hit Mrs. Newcomber with the baseball bat, right?" I asked.

"You've got it in one," said Robbie. "Thanks to that card you found with Allen's phone number, the Belleville police were able to shake his tree. Once he realized he was on the hook for Trudy's disappearance, he was more than willing to rat out his mentor."

"Thank God," said Mert. "For his manifold and great blessings. Because if Allen hadn't tattled on Fred Ernest, Trudy might not have made it outta there alive."

One week later…

"I baked a batch of pumpkin cookies." Rebekkah opened a Tupperware container. "They're for my going away party this evening, but you can sample them, Kiki. I know how you insist on making sure they're worthy of our customers."

"You bet I do!" I bit into one and moaned with joy.

"You aren't really going away," Dodie said to her daughter. "Not exactly. This is just the crop where you'll take a bow and exit stage right as our Sales Mangler."

I giggled. So Dodie *had* caught the typo.

"Even though you're moving out of your parents' house, we'll still need you at the store," I said as I "sampled" my second cookie eagerly. I take my quality control job very seriously

"School first, then family, and finally the store." Dodie bit into her third cookie. Every quality control officer needs a good second in command. Dodie was right there with me, sampling the merchandise.

She and I had decided that we would limit Rebekkah's "helping at the store" to specific activities where she couldn't ruin any craft supplies. Otherwise, Rebekkah typically trashed more paper and products than a springtime flooding of the Mississippi River.

"I can't wait to get my own place off campus in U City. My parents and I need a break from each other," Rebekkah said.

"Your father and I love you, but you're probably right." Dodie's smile was colored with sadness.

It was time for Rebekkah to go back to school and to get out of Dodie and Horace's collective hair. Or what they had left of it. Their daughter had applied and been accepted to Washington University, with the goal of finishing her undergraduate degree and then attending the George Warren Brown School of Social

Work as a graduate student.

I was delighted that we'd found a good solution for Rebekkah, and I was thrilled because Clancy would be picking up more hours. Having my friend around would make it much easier for me to put up with Bama.

"By the way." Rebekkah slung an arm around her mother's neck. "I called Rabbi Sarah yesterday. She told me there's no prohibition against burying Jews with tattoos in Jewish cemeteries."

Dodie rolled her eyes to the heavens and muttered a prayer in Hebrew.

"You aren't planning your own burial already, are you?" I asked Rebekkah. "You're awfully young."

"I promise that I'm not going anywhere until I help you prep for your crop tonight. You do need help, don't you?" Rebekkah asked.

"Of course I do. I'm going to teach a couple of new Zentangle designs and show our students how to use the designs in jewelry." I didn't bother to add that after all the 24/7 news about Allen Lever and Fred Ernest's killing spree, I hungered for more zen in my life. As it was, I had nightmares about that stupid wood chipper.

Rebekkah must have read my mind. "What did I hear on the news? Twelve women?"

"Twelve and counting." Clancy walked up behind us. Because this was Rebekkah's last official crop, Clancy had decided to join us for the evening. As usual, Bama bowed out, explaining that she had another commitment.

Clancy continued, "Part of the deal to avoid the death penalty was that Alfred Ernest would come clean on all the women he'd killed. His career as a serial killer had started before he got poor Allen Lever involved. I have a hunch the number of victims might grow."

"There's Marla's death, too," I said. "Fred Ernest is responsible for that." Shortly after Detweiler and Hadcho had arrested her son, Marla Lever suffered another massive stroke and died in the hospital. In my heart of hearts, I believed that Marla finally knew she could move on, and so she did. Clancy, Dodie, and I had attended the memorial service for our friend. As we stood by Marla's open grave, I prayed the poor woman would finally get a measure of closure. The death of her youngest child, Anthony, had left a gaping hole in Marla's psyche that the years had never healed. She had tried to fill that pain by hoarding. Now Marla and the child she'd lost would be reunited.

Was it possible that Dodie considered her own death as a chance to see Nathan again? That would be a comforting thought. Maybe it made the possibility of cancer more bearable. Whatever she was thinking, she steadfastly refused to discuss seeing a doctor about the lump she'd found. Every attempt to push her to make an appointment had resulted in her getting angry with me. Reluctantly, I'd come to the conclusion there was nothing more I could do.

While I was thinking about Dodie, the conversation had moved along.

"There's also the vandalizing of your home." Clancy handed me a napkin and pointed to crumbs on my face. "Can you believe that Fred Ernest talked Allen Lever into doing that? Talk about being under someone's spell!"

"That's how it must have been for years," I said. "Robbie says it's not that uncommon in homicidal duos. There's always a leader and a follower. Fred would tell Allen what to do, and Allen looked up to the man, so he'd trot off and do it. That's why Allen agreed to meet Trudy in the parking lot over in Soulard. Fred didn't trust her to keep her mouth shut after she'd snooped around at his house. As an insurance policy, he told her that Allen had mentioned he'd love to take Trudy out."

"She was so eager to find Mr. Right that she kept chasing Mr.

Wrong," said Clancy.

An uncomfortable silence followed. All my friends were aware that I'd told Detweiler I didn't want any more contact with him. He wasn't Mr. Wrong, but he was Mr. Unavailable. Telling him that I'd rather he not stop by my house or the store was the hardest thing I've done in years, but I did it. Dodie, Sheila, and Clancy backed me up in my decision. They all pledged that if the handsome cop dropped in and tried to ask about me, they'd nip the conversation in the bud.

"Did Mert ever get paid?" asked Dodie.

"Yes, but she had to hire an attorney to threaten Ali Timmons."

The Lever house in Ladue had since been razed. Instead of building two houses, the Timmons sold it to a developer.

Pamela Bertolli told me all about it, adding, "They never did hire that fancy agent after all. He refused to work with them. As soon as the check clears, they're moving to another state."

My boss promised we'd never have to do another crop at a remote location unless I had the chance to vet the place.

"That reminds me," said Clancy, "Remember how I got ink on my purse the day we showed up at Marla Lever's house? Look at it now." Where there'd once been a plain white leather hobo bag, there was now a cool purse covered with designs done in black ink—a Zentangle dream!

"A crime solved, an item repurposed, and—" I plucked out the newest member of my family out of his cat carrier "—a kitten rescued. All is well, isn't it?"

I did my best to smile. Okay, so the guy of my dreams was married. I still had reasons to be happy. Martin snuggled under my chin, and the ache in my heart eased a little.

~The End~

Kiki's story continues in ***Photo, Snap, Shot: Book #4 in the Kiki Lowenstein Mystery Series***. Available from Amazon.com

The Backstory: An Author's Note

Hoarding is a recognized disorder where a person has trouble letting go of material objects. As a crafter, I can relate. In fact, in the UK, they call people like me "paper strokers," because we enjoy looking at our stash so much that we're hesitant to use it.

However, Marla's problem is much more severe. In fact, I got the idea for this book after I read a letter written by the daughter of a hoarder in which she explained how devastating her mother's illness was. Research has shown that hoarding impacts 2 to 6 percent of the adult population. It's more prevalent in men than in women. It runs in families, often starts when a person is a teen, and can be a response to a brain injury.

When people decide to hoard animals, there's a secondary layer of misery, because the animals often suffer. Many hoarders are delusional, unable to see that they are actually mistreating the animals they claim to love. As you've read in this book, municipalities have trouble passing laws that keep hoarding (and animal hoarding) in check. When a family member becomes a hoarder, there's little the rest of the family can do. Some therapists suggest "tough love," where the hoarder is warned that no one will visit until the mess is cleaned up. Other counselors work alongside the hoarder, helping him or her to become less emotionally invested in things. On occasion, the only solution is to remove the hoarder from the house, clear everything out, and then return the hoarder. This is useful because the mess can be so overwhelming that a hoarder can't function, much less make good decisions about getting rid of junk.

The bottom line is that hoarding is a mental disorder, usually an inappropriate response to stress.

Our Gift to You

Kiki and I have a special gift for you. We have a file filled with recipes and extras that go along with this book. If you send an email to IRDBonus@JoannaSlan.com, our computer guru will automatically send the file to you. Furthermore, we will add you to our online newsletter mailing list at no charge. Of course, you can drop off at any time, but you won't want to. Each month we send you a list of free and discounted books and other goodies. You'll see why people can't wait to get it!

If you have any trouble accessing the free bonus or with the newsletter, you can contact my assistant, Sally Lippert, at SALFL27@att.net.

With gratitude from your friend,

Joanna

P.S. If you enjoyed this book, I hope you'll consider writing a review and posting it on Amazon, Barnes & Noble, Kobo, or Goodreads. In today's crowded marketplace, more and more of us turn to reviews to make purchasing decisions. (I know I always read all the reviews before I buy. Even the bad ones, because they are enlightening.) Your opinion matters. In addition, I read reviews to get a better understanding of what you, my readers, like and enjoy. So…thanks in advance.

P.P.S. I'd like to introduce you to a few of my author friends. Go to http://bit.ly/2HH, and you'll be able to download a copy of ***Happy Homicides 2: Crimes of the Heart*** absolutely free. It's a collection of short mysteries by a variety of authors.

The Kiki Lowenstein Mystery Series

Every scrapbook tells a story. Memories of friends, family, and …
murder? You'll want to read the Kiki Lowenstein books in order:

0. ***Love, Die, Neighbor (The Prequel)***
1. ***Paper, Scissors, Death***
2. ***Cut, Crop & Die***
3. ***Ink, Red, Dead***
4. ***Photo, Snap, Shot***
5. ***Make, Take, Murder***
6. ***Ready, Scrap, Shoot***
7. ***Picture, Perfect, Corpse***
8. ***Group, Photo, Grave***
9. ***Killer, Paper, Cut***
10. ***Handmade, Holiday, Homicide***
11. ***Shotgun, Wedding, Bells***
12. ***Glue, Baby, Gone***

I've also written nearly 40 short stories that go between the books.

The Cara Mia Delgatto Mystery Series

A new series that's a spin-off of the Kiki Lowenstein books. If you believe in second chances, you're going to love Cara Mia and her friends. Here are those books in order:

1. *Tear Down & Die*
2. *Kicked to the Curb*
3. *All Washed Up*

And yes, there are short stories that go with these, too. (I can't help myself!)

About the Author...

National bestselling and award-winning author Joanna Campbell Slan has written 30 books, including both fiction and non-fiction works. Her first non-fiction book, *Using Stories and Humor: Grab Your Audience,* was endorsed by Toastmasters International, and lauded by Benjamin Netanyahu's speechwriter. She's the author of three mystery series. Her first novel – *Paper, Scissors, Death (Book #1 in the Kiki Lowenstein Mystery Series)* – was shortlisted for the Agatha Award. Recently she released *Glue, Baby, Gone (Book #12 in the Kiki Lowenstein Mystery Series).* Her first historical mystery – *Death of a Schoolgirl: The Jane Eyre Chronicles* – won the Daphne du Maurier Award of Excellence. Her contemporary series set in Florida continues this year with *All Washed Up (Cara Mia Delgatto Mystery #3).* In addition to writing fiction, she edits the Happy Homicides Anthologies and has begun the Dollhouse Décor & More series of "how to" books for dollhouse miniaturists. Recently, one of her short stories was accepted for inclusion in the prestigious *Chesapeake Crimes: Fur, Feathers, and Felonies* anthology. When she isn't banging away at the keyboard, Joanna keeps busy walking her Havanese puppy Jax and watching her family's League of Legends Team Dignitas on Twitch. Her husband, David, owns Steinway Piano Gallery-DC. The Slans make their home in Jupiter Island, Florida.

- Visit Joanna at – http://www.JoannaSlan.com
- Email her at – JCSlan@JoannaSlan.com
- Join her community of readers for fun, special offers, contests, and more at – http://bit.ly/JCSGroup
- Send her mail through the USPS at –Joanna Slan / 9307 SE Olympus Street / Hobe Sound FL 33455 USA

~*~

Do You Like Free and Discounted Books?

Who doesn't? Be sure to sign up for Joanna's free online newsletter, Deals and Steals. Each month she features free and discounted books, recipes, and other freebies. Go to http://www.JoannaSlan.com or contact Sally at SALFL27@att.net
to sign up.